Blaze®

Dear Reader,

Welcome back to the Uniformly Hot! miniseries. You first met Captain Sam Brody in *All the Right Moves*. Now he has his own story in *To the Limit*.

Being a fighter pilot is all Sam has ever wanted. He's worked hard for the privilege of strapping himself into an F-16. But something has gone terribly wrong. The good news? He's been assigned to Holloman AFB. An old friend lives there, teaching at a campus on base.

Emma Lockwood is finally content. After her fighter-pilot husband, Danny, was killed three years ago, she never thought she'd be happy again, but she loves her job, has made good friends and might even consider dating.

But when Sam calls, she's not even sure she wants to meet him for dinner. The secrets she's kept from Sam, from everyone, could hurt them both. She's always liked Sam. Too much....

I hope you enjoy Emma and Sam's journey as much as I did. Visit with me at www.joleigh.com or @Jo_Leigh on Twitter.

All my best,

Jo Leigh

To the Limit

Jo Leigh

H HARLEQUIN® BLAZE™

Recycling programs
for this product may
not exist in your area.

ISBN-13: 978-0-373-79764-6

TO THE LIMIT

Copyright © 2013 by Jolie Kramer

Printed in U.S.A.

www.Harlequin.com

ABOUT THE AUTHOR

Jo Leigh is from Los Angeles and always thought she'd end up living in Manhattan. So how did she end up in Utah, in a tiny town with a terrible internet connection, being bossed around by a house full of rescued cats and dogs? What the heck, she says, predictability is boring. Jo has written more than forty-five novels for Harlequin Books. Visit her website at www.joleigh.com or contact her at joleigh@joleigh.com.

Books by Jo Leigh

HARLEQUIN BLAZE

To get the inside scoop on Harlequin Blaze and its talented writers, be sure to check out blazeauthors.com.

Other titles by this author available in ebook format. Don't miss any of our special offers. Write to us at the following address for information on our newest releases.

Harlequin Reader Service
U.S.: 3010 Walden Ave., P.O. Box 1325, Buffalo, NY 14269
Canadian: P.O. Box 609, Fort Erie, Ont. L2A 5X

1

THE MOTEL ROOM looked as tired as Captain Sam Brody felt after his endless flight from Sumter Air Force Base in South Carolina to Alamogordo, New Mexico. Of course, the bachelor party he'd been to last night might have something to do with his exhaustion. Seemed everyone Sam knew was hooking up or getting married.

He tossed his duffel on the garish bedspread and joined it a moment later, glad to be sitting on something relatively soft. The transport plane he'd hitched a ride with had been incredibly uncomfortable with all the turbulence, and the taxi he'd hired at Holloman Air Force Base had evidently been cobbled together with chewing gum and shocks made from empty soup cans. His car, packed with all he owned in the world, was due to arrive in a few days. In the meantime, he'd find an off-base furnished apartment.

He had ten days of leave ahead of him before he started life at the new base, with a new wing, new line of command, new everything. The only thing he knew for sure about moving to this small military town was that someone he used to know lived here. The wife of an old friend.

Sam shut down that line of thought quickly. He was too damn tired to let his memories sidetrack him. What he needed was some food, a beer and a bed. He opened up the drawer of the nightstand and pulled out the phone book. It was about a quarter of the size of the one in Texas. He sure as hell wouldn't miss the weather, although he'd probably miss the humidity in the middle of a dry-as-dust summer in the desert.

Most of the delivery foods he found were pizza, so he picked a familiar chain. After ordering a large cheese, he wasn't shocked at the laugh he got when he asked if beer was on the menu. But he'd seen a market a block away, so no worries.

Before he put the phone book away, he went to the white pages but Emma wasn't listed. It wasn't surprising. Most likely she didn't have a landline. Clicking through his cell phone's contacts he found Emma Lockwood. He hadn't deleted the listing in the three years since Danny had died. Of course he had her Alamogordo address, but it was a long shot that she still lived in the same town, let alone the same house. She probably didn't even have the same number. He could always delete everything later if it turned out Emma wasn't interested in…whatever.

He didn't have time to shower and make a beer run before his dinner arrived, so he settled for washing his face before walking to the market. The September evening felt good on his skin despite the fact that it was still in the eighties, but he'd have to get used to the smell. Randolph Air Force Base always had a hint of mesquite in the air. Just like the wind had carried the ocean back in his hometown of Seal Beach, California.

He shoved his hands in his pockets as he strolled, checking out the scenery. Nothing much to it. He could have been in any inner-city area littered with billboards and graffiti on brick walls, people walking with purpose from the stores that weren't boarded up.

There was a lot more to Alamogordo than this neighborhood, but he didn't mind staying here for a few days. Odds were he wouldn't run into any other pilots. Any other officers at all. Which was a good thing for the time being.

Transitions were part of air force life, but they never got easier for Sam. At heart, he was a homebody, which made no sense for a man who loved to fly as much as he did. But he'd grown up moving a lot as his mother searched for employment. Retirement after he'd gotten his twenty years would be a welcome relief. He'd find himself a comfortable house, something with enough land around it that he wouldn't hear the neighbors. He'd have a yard and a couple of rescue dogs, and he'd put down roots there. A real home. Hopefully not on his own.

He wondered if Emma still wore her blond hair in that ponytail. Danny'd sure liked to tug on that, even though it made her cross. He'd always been an overgrown kid. Hell of a fun guy, generous, too. They'd all shared so much laughter: Danny and John Devlin and then Emma Taylor, the waitress at the Rusty Nail bar and diner a couple of blocks away from the Air Force Academy. He'd loved those years. The three guys had bonded quickly, shared a house that wasn't exactly the Ritz. They'd all wanted to fly F-16s and they'd all worked their asses off to get there.

But sometimes the studying got to be too much and they'd head off to the Rusty Nail. Danny had seen Emma, and she'd seen him right back. It was all over but the paperwork from that night on. They'd gotten married a year later, in Danny's senior year.

God, she'd been so pretty. Slender and delicate. Little wrists, long fingers. She always looked perfect, even in those terrible T-shirts she wore back then. Crazy stuff, big writing over her chest. Mostly with pictures of heavy metal bands. Which she didn't actually listen to. She just liked the shirts.

He didn't realize he was smiling until he saw his reflection in the convenience store's door. Leave it to Emma to make a horrible day better. He used to think Danny was the luckiest son of a bitch he'd ever met. Until he wasn't.

The little market not only carried his favorite beer, but a cooler and ice, so he bought himself a six-pack, some beef jerky and a box of Pop-Tarts for the morning. Nothing he could do about coffee except get himself to a diner as quickly as possible, because, screw it, he was not drinking microwaved instant. Not for anything.

The pizza arrived twelve minutes after he got back to the motel, and it was hot enough to burn the roof of his mouth. The TV wasn't as much of a success. There weren't many channels that worked, but one of them was ESPN, so that was okay, even if half the picture was snow.

He woke up the next morning to the sound of the TV, still dressed, his second beer half-empty on the nightstand. The day ahead would look better after a shower and a decent breakfast. At least, he hoped so.

WITH FIVE MINUTES LEFT of Emma Lockwood's creative writing class, all fourteen of her students had their heads bent, the sound of clicking laptop keys a staccato symphony she knew by heart. She'd given them a writing assignment when they'd come into class, a simple mood piece, but she'd asked them to write it in a genre that wasn't their own. So Mrs. Dealy, who was taking the class for the third time because she loved to write but didn't have the discipline to do it without deadlines, was tackling science fiction, even though she wrote love stories. Jared, one of her freshmen straight from Holloman High School, was extremely brave, writing his piece in the style of Raymond Chandler, a real hard-boiled mystery.

Emma wished all of her students were as enthusiastic as the ones in this class. But so many of her courses were merely stepping stones to an associate degree. Most of the students would go on to get their bachelor degrees at New Mexico State, but for some, this would be the end of the education line.

She sat on the edge of her desk with two minutes on the clock. "Okay, everyone," she said. "Please continue working on the assignments throughout the week, and we'll hear them during Friday's class."

Reggie Porter, one of the several veterans who'd come back from the war and was using the G.I. Bill to help him get a better job, raised his hand, although he didn't wait for her to acknowledge it. "How long are these supposed to be?"

"Between four and nine thousand words."

"So there goes football night."

"It'll be exciting," Emma said and smiled at his deadpan expression. "Just think of how much you learned during the first-person exercise. Broadening your horizons is never a waste of time unless you let it be. Give it your best shot. Ingenuity counts. Make the genre clear in the story itself."

The bell went off and the post-class shuffle of laptop cases and backpacks began. They were in their second month of the fall semester, so there was conversation among them, mostly about the work, but sometimes about other things. She was glad. She wanted her classes to be enlivened by dialogue off the page as well as on.

After cleaning the blackboards and making sure everything in the room was tidy, she got her purse and her books and walked the semiquiet halls to the faculty lounge in the Lower Campus Classroom building at Holloman Air Force

Base. The sound of jets taking off and landing had become background noise after living close to them for so long, not just here, but in Colorado and Utah. They'd never stopped reminding her of Danny, but at least now the thrum of the engines didn't feel like a punishment.

Sharon Keeler was at the coffee machine, staring at the sludge at the bottom of the stained pot. Sharon was part of the arts faculty staff, but she was mostly concerned with her drama department. They were doing *As You Like It* this fall, and she was in a tizzy about costumes and lighting and the lack of much discernible talent among the students.

"You in for a late night?" Emma asked.

Sharon nodded, her long dark hair looking worse for wear since this morning. On the plus side, she'd worn her favorite cow-themed earrings, a sure sign she'd been in a good mood this morning. "Campus-planning committee meeting. You want to come?"

Emma held back a laugh because she didn't want to be cruel. "Sorry, I have lesson plans, grading book reports and laundry. I know, scintillating."

"What's scintillating?"

Emma and Sharon turned when Gary Lyden walked in. Gary wasn't particularly great-looking, but he was a runner and a health enthusiast and he put himself together really well. Somewhat new—it was his second year in the math department—he was an Idaho transplant. Mostly, he was nice. A solid guy who was good with his students and easy to be around. Emma and he were becoming better and better friends, as it turned out.

"Are you coming tonight?" Sharon asked. "I know it's Tuesday and you have that Habitat meeting later, but none of the teachers RSVP'd and besides, it wasn't my fault. It was the only night the parents could come, and I'm desperate."

"Really?" he asked, raising his eyebrows. "How desperate?"

"Fine, I'll bake you an entire batch of granola fruit bars all for yourself. Well, not this week, but soon. Good enough?"

Gary rubbed his hands together. "Those are damn good snacks. So yes, I'm in. But don't think you can talk me into helping with your scenery. I'm into theory, not practice." He looked to Emma. "You can't make it?"

"Not tonight. In fact, I'm going to actually leave the base before 7:00 p.m. I think it might be the first time that's happened since the semester started."

"They do keep chipping away at us," Sharon said as she went to the sink to wash out the coffeepot. "I should quit. Get myself a career that pays better money."

"Or at least one where the out-of-pocket expenses aren't so high," Gary said. He came closer to Emma and touched the back of her arm, but only for a second. "You want to run tomorrow?"

"Hmm…" She should. The exercise was helping with her energy dips. They'd been heading out for a couple months now, going to the high school track before school started on Mondays and Thursdays, but she wasn't sure yet if she wanted it to become anything more regular. "To be honest, I could use a decent morning's sleep since I have a later class. Sorry."

"No problem. Thursday then?"

"Good. Yes. Thursday." She went to her mail cubby, which was conveniently placed at the bottom of the stack, and got her notices and flyers and a couple of letters from the school district. She'd look at them later.

Behind her, the door swung open again, only this time there were several teachers coming in, seemingly in the middle of a fierce discussion about the merits of soccer over football.

She waited until the doorway was clear, then waved her goodbyes. Her phone rang just as she reached the exit to the parking lot. The name on the caller ID stole her breath and her grace. She stumbled, but thankfully didn't fall.

Sam Brody. She hadn't seen him since shortly after Danny died. But she'd thought of him. More often than she should have, considering. But not so much lately.

She almost let the call go to voice mail, but it was so out of the blue that she couldn't stand it. She pressed the key. "Hello?"

"Emma," he said, and his voice sent a shiver skittering down her back.

"Sam. It's been a while."

"I know. Too long."

She nodded, but held her tongue.

"Hey, I'm just calling to let you know that we're neighbors."

"What?" Emma looked around, conscious of how loud she'd been. "What do you mean?"

"I've been assigned to Holloman."

"Starting when?"

"Now. I'm on leave, though, for the next ten days. Enough time to find an apartment. Get my bearings."

"So you're here now?"

"Yeah. I'm here."

"Oh. That's great. That's…great."

"We'll see, but then, you know how it is, being transferred. A real crapshoot."

"I can give you some pointers if you need them," she said, wincing the moment the words were out of her mouth. It had been a reflex. They'd been friends once. Certainly Sam had been one of Danny's closest. They'd gone through a lot together, but after the crash, both Sam and John had stopped calling. Not their fault. She'd made it clear she wanted some space. Especially from Sam.

"That'd be great," he said. "I was thinking maybe you'd like to go out, have some dinner with me?"

"Tonight?"

"Not necessarily," he said, although he spoke so quickly it was clear that was just what he'd meant. "I'm sure you're busy. With a…your life. Here. You teaching?"

"Yeah."

"Wow. Great."

She thought about telling him dinner wasn't such a good idea, but the words wouldn't come. She was walking now, nowhere in particular, down some stairs, past rows of cars. "How about tomorrow night?"

He sighed. "Tomorrow night would be perfect. You'll have to say where, though. I've got no idea what's around here."

"Are you staying at the base?"

"Nope. But I'm close to it. So how about you text me the name and location of your favorite restaurant. I'll meet you there. Tomorrow. Seven okay?"

"Yeah. Seven's fine." Her heels clicked on the concrete during a lull in jet traffic as she slowed to a standstill. "It'll be good to see you again."

"It will. Don't forget to save the number, now."

"I won't."

"Okay. Have a good one."

"You, too," she said, then hung up. When she pressed the keys to put him in her contacts, her hand shook a bit. Probably the surprise. Or maybe it was the surge of adrenaline that had hit her hard.

She'd loved Danny. She had. But there'd always been a spark between her and Sam. She knew he'd felt it. Their collective discomfort had been masked by the typical craziness that was life back then, especially after they'd been sent to Randolph AFB to finish training and she'd been working forty hours a week as a waitress while getting her degree at Texas A&M. The four of them had still managed to hang out together, and to get into all kinds of mischief. God, pilots were a breed unto themselves. Cocky, stupidly brave and loyal to a fault.

Sam had never said a word. She'd never given Danny a reason to be concerned. But the attraction had been real and had run deep. She couldn't imagine what it would be like to see him again. Three years had gone by. Enough time for him to have fallen for someone. To be married, even. Maybe the wife was selling their old place. The idea tightened her chest, which was ridiculous. It made sense that Sam would be married now. He was thirty-three, more handsome than was fair and a good guy. Really good. He'd have been snapped up in a heartbeat.

Although the air force life wasn't for the weak, even for a spouse. It was a different universe from anything she'd experienced before, and she'd meant to get as far away from that universe as she could. And yet, here she was, in the last place Danny had been assigned. He'd never even gotten to the base. She'd come ahead to get them settled. He'd died a thousand miles away.

Sam, though. He must have been assigned to the F-22 Raptor, which aside from the remotely piloted aircraft was the largest unit. It was a hotshot plane for the best of the best. She wondered where John was stationed. If he'd gotten married. She had her doubts. He'd loved being a bachelor fighter pilot.

She'd spent a considerable amount of time with those guys over the years. They'd treated her very nicely, not at all like a Yoko. In fact, they'd gone out of their way to make her feel welcome. But a lot had changed since then. Odds were she'd regret tomorrow night's dinner. Still, she wasn't going to back out.

Maybe it was time she told someone the truth about what had been going on right before Danny died.

She pressed a hand to her jittery stomach.

Or maybe not.

2

EMMA HAD SECOND THOUGHTS a moment before she entered Stella Vita, the downtown restaurant she'd chosen for the reunion. In reality, there weren't that many choices in Alamogordo. It probably would have been better to take Sam to her favorite Mexican place and then show him what he'd need to get around town, but she wanted wine with the food, not beer. Not tonight.

She took a seat facing the door, feeling more nervous than she had on her first date with Danny. She'd changed a lot in the years since she and Sam had seen each other. Her hair was shorter, a longish pixie cut that was meant to be messy-looking, which made getting ready in the morning less of a nightmare. Also her hair was lighter now than when he'd last seen her.

Her fingers went to the wisps at her nape, where she tugged on a stray curl. She'd probably left it too messy, and he'd think she was making some kind of statement, but no, that wasn't like Sam. He'd never noticed her hair all that much, although he'd always commented about her T-shirts. A quick look at her watch told her it was too late to run to the restroom to check her do now. Besides, she could guarantee Sam hadn't been changing clothes and agonizing over his makeup…. That made her grin. Sam wasn't exactly the makeup type.

He was effortlessly gorgeous. Tall, well built, strong jaw, light brown hair that looked blond by the end of summer and a smile that turned women to putty.

Needing that glass of wine, she glanced around for the waitress just as he walked in. Sam wasn't in uniform. Even though he'd said he was on leave, it still surprised her to see him in jeans. Or was it the way he looked at her that set her heart racing?

Eyes wide, his gaze stayed on her face as if she was the best thing he'd ever laid eyes on. When he didn't move, just continued to stare, the urge to look away was strong, but there was nothing else she wanted to see. Finally, he smiled and headed to their table.

She stood. The closer he got, the more memories he sparked. The way he'd first introduced himself all those years ago by standing up, holding out his hand, as if she'd been someone important instead of the waitress taking his order. She'd already been flustered meeting Danny and John, and then Sam…tall at six-one, the most amazing eyelashes she'd ever seen on a man, and oh, his voice was all deep and rumbly even when all he was saying was "I'd like a beer, please."

He hadn't changed much. Still broad-shouldered and slim-hipped, he looked so fine in his jeans and a tan linen shirt that the *thing* started, the strange sensation that felt as if she needed a really deep breath even though she knew there wasn't enough air in the world. She looked up to meet his gaze, inches away now and real in a way she hadn't been able to conjure even with her vivid imagination.

He smelled like Sam. Like the old Sam. Her friend.

"Oh, hell," he said, and he pulled her into a hug that practically swallowed her whole. She didn't mind. The heat from outside was still on him as she pressed her cheek against his chest. Her arms went low and wrapped around him tightly.

She only realized he'd leaned into her hair when she felt him whisper her name. It made her smile and it made her sad in equal measure. This reunion was so filled with baggage they might crumble under the weight.

Before it got weird he let her go. "How is it possible you've gotten more beautiful?"

She blushed, of course. "Look who's talking. You should quit this flying nonsense and model underwear. You'd make millions."

The way he rolled his eyes was like a jolt into the past. It was going to be a rocky evening, she could tell. She hoped it was worth it. She liked Sam too much to have to avoid him. Not that he'd do anything on purpose, but that last year, whenever she'd seen him…

He had his hand on the back of her chair, and after she sat, he joined her, smiling. "This looks like a nice restaurant," he said, looking everywhere but at her. "The walls are very…"

She glanced at his fingers. No ring. Didn't necessarily mean anything. "Mustard. I think that's the color you're looking for."

He nodded. "It works, though."

"It does," she said, hoping he wasn't feeling too awkward. "The food's even better than the decor. If I remember correctly, you're a steak man."

He nodded and leaned forward as if to say something, but the waitress showed up with menus and a wine list.

"Hey, I'm Crystal. Can I start you off with something to drink?"

Sam glanced down at the wines. "You still like merlot?"

She nodded. "That'd be great."

Sam ordered a bottle and the waitress left, which was good because the woman had been staring hard at Sam, and not just because he was ordering. Emma had seen Crystal check out Sam's chest. The big inhale hadn't been very subtle and neither had the swipe of her tongue across her bottom lip.

"So," Sam said, his gaze firmly on his open menu. "Steak, huh?"

"Everything I've had here is good."

He nodded. She knew only because she kept sneaking her own glances while she tried to focus on the entrées. Clearly, this evening out had been a mistake. The awkward was inching toward nerve-racking, and she doubted things would improve. They had been step-friends who'd been attracted to each other. Right there was a recipe for disaster. Danny had been their anchor, and she knew Sam wouldn't want to bring him up, and she sure as hell didn't, but what was left? The weather?

"It sure is dry out here," he said. "I just came from San Antonio and that place was a sauna. This dry air's going to take some getting used to."

"Moisturizer," Emma said. "Get a great big old bottle and use it every day. Seriously. You'll dry out like a chili pepper if you don't. I go through tons of it myself."

"I'll do that," he said. "Thanks.

She stared at the menu again, chanting silently for the wine to arrive.

"San Antonio?" she said at the same second he asked, "What are you teaching?"

He put down his menu and said, "Hell, Emma, you know pretty much everything I've been doing…. It's the air force. No personal changes worth noting. My family's fine. I've been to Iraq and Afghanistan, but it was as easy as active duty in a war zone can be. Frankly, I'd love to hear about your job, about this town. But mostly about you."

She knew Sam well enough to know that his little speech was meant to make her more comfortable, but it backfired. All the times he'd gone the extra mile to be kind to her when things had been rough between her and Danny came barreling over her like an oncoming tide. He'd been a good friend. To both of them. Always ready to lend a nonjudgmental ear. He'd encouraged her to continue her education no matter where Danny got transferred, get her teaching degree, which was the best advice ever.

"Okay," she said, hoping some small talk would put her at ease. "I teach at the community college. English. Which includes creative writing, rhetoric and composition, and some literature courses. It's great, though, because the school is on the base, and we get all kinds of students. A lot of vets, of course, and freshmen, but we have a big contingent of adults who've been displaced because of the economy and they're looking to broaden their chances of getting work. We've even got a gray-haired brigade of older folks who just love to learn, so…" She shrugged. "It's challenging and fun to try and meet all their needs."

"From what I hear, it's getting harder and harder to be a teacher. Lack of funding an issue for you?"

She nodded but the wine came, and she didn't respond until she and Sam had their glasses filled. "There's not a lot of money in the school budget, though we're better off than some other state universities. I feel sorry for the elementary and middle schools, but of course they have the military wives doing some serious fund-raising for them."

Sam put his glass down, nodding. "They're a force to be reckoned with."

Emma closed her eyes, wishing she could stop the memories of her own days as Danny's wife. She'd been the worst air force wife ever, even before they'd been married. College and a full-time job left no time for any of the group activities that had been available to her. When she had a break to relax, she spent it with Danny alone or with the guys. Fishing trips, hiking, having too much beer and pizza when there wasn't anything better to do.

She opened her eyes to find Sam watching her. She managed a smile. "I didn't really get it until after," she said. "About the wives."

"Hey, you were busy. No one expected you to do anything but love Danny."

She grabbed her glass and probably would have drained it if Crystal hadn't come back to take their orders. Once that was done, Emma said, "Alamogordo is pretty interesting, if you're willing to do a bit of traveling. There's great stuff nearby. Carlsbad Caverns, the White Sands National Monument and the space museum, and oh, there's a pistachio farm, which is nice…well, if you like pistachios. We're not far from El Paso, either. There are lots of things to do.…" She felt the heat in her cheeks, but his smile wasn't mocking. In fact, it was as warm as her blush.

"You've sold me," he said.

She sighed, wishing she could disappear under the table. "And it's a dry heat."

SAM LAUGHED and felt the last of the tightness in his shoulders dissipate. Although he had to be careful not to stare too often. Emma hadn't changed very much. Shorter, blonder hair, makeup now when she used to wear nothing but bright red lipstick and sunscreen. He knew that second thing only because she'd told him. She'd told him a lot of weird stuff back then, and he remembered thinking she needed a BFF. Bad. Not that she'd crossed any lines or anything, but he hadn't known what to say when she'd asked if she should streak her hair, or if she could get away with wearing yellow. He'd just said the kind thing and hoped for the best.

Truth was, he always thought she looked great. Every time. Even when she'd wake up from one of their camping trips with terrible bed head. He didn't care. He'd just been happy she was there.

"Those folks are so lucky to have you for a teacher," he said.

She looked at him skeptically, those almond-shaped eyes narrowed and her lips pressed together. "That's very nice of you to say, but you've never seen me teach. I could be horrible."

"Not a chance," he said. "Hold on a sec." He reached into the pocket of his jeans and pulled out his iPod Nano. After unwinding his earbuds, he held them out to her, and she put them up next to her ears. Then he pressed Play.

A few seconds later, her mouth and her eyes widened with such excitement, he might have just given her keys to a Ferrari. "Still?" she asked.

"Yep. I'm hooked. Just don't spread it around. I don't need a whole new base knowing that I listen to classical music."

Grinning like a nut, she listened for a bit, then handed him back the iPod. "You've expanded your repertoire."

Sam shrugged. "A bit. I still like the American composers, though."

"No reason not to. Although a little Bach never hurt anyone."

"You and Bach. Jeez, woman. That's so eighteenth century."

Her laughter fixed everything that had been wrong all day. Going to Holloman, hearing that his car wouldn't arrive until Friday, the crappy coffee he'd had this morning.

The food came and the waitress gave him the look again. A pretty blatant invitation considering he was sitting across from a woman. A beautiful woman at that.

Dismissing the whole business, he waited until Emma picked up her utensils and started working on her duck before he dug into his rib eye, and the whole time the two of them were grinning as though they shared a fantastic secret. He supposed they did.

There was a maturity about her now, even though it had been only three years since he'd seen her. Being a widow left its mark, although there was nothing obvious about the change. He'd seen the old Emma for a few seconds there, listening to the music. He'd like to see it again.

"What about your family," he said. "Anything new there?"

She shook her head. "They're still in Philly, doing fine. My sister had a baby five months ago, so that's nice."

He finished off his wine and topped them both up. "Any significant others?"

Her gaze darted away as she shook her head. "No one. I'm not... I'm not really looking."

"Right." He had no business feeling pleased. None. "Me, neither. But I have been getting my bad self down with some midnight bowling."

That made her laugh again. "Midnight bowling?" she asked, after sipping some water. "You're not even joking. How did that happen?"

"A crazy-ass pilot, what else? He was dating this civilian, and there was a local bowling alley that did late-night stuff, with black lights and cheap beer, and lots of folks showed up. A group of us went when we had a chance. I know it sounds stupid, but it was fun."

Emma looked around the dining room, either in search of the waitress or to make sure she wouldn't be overheard.

When she turned back to him she leaned closer. "We do the bowling thing here, too."

"Really? You any good?"

"No, I kind of suck at it, but we have a league. It's mostly teachers. Not a lot of airmen show up, at least not on our league night. But you should come sometime. We're always missing somebody. You could be my ringer."

"I'm not that good."

"Can you break a hundred?"

He grinned. "Most of the time."

"You're in," she said, but then her smile froze. A few seconds later she continued eating her asparagus, but something had changed. Most likely she hadn't intended to see him again and was wishing she'd kept her mouth shut.

He wanted to ask her if he made things too painful. If she could look at him without thinking of Danny. If she had known Sam had compared all other women to her, and they'd always fallen short. Yeah, that wouldn't be awkward and inappropriate. "Other than bowling, what else keeps you entertained when you're not at school?"

"I don't know how entertaining it is, but usually I'm working on lesson plans, or tutoring, or like now I'm helping to put together a funnel-cake booth for the upcoming Fall Festival. Oh, and my big thrill for the month…I'm lending a hand with making the costumes for a play at the school."

Sam smiled at her mock enthusiasm. "You can sew?"

"I've learned, although I'm no Martha Stewart. Thankfully, I'm mostly patching up or changing costumes that have been used before, so it's not that hard. I don't mind. I listen to podcasts or audiobooks while I'm working on them."

She might not have gotten married again, but she had built a life for herself. Friends and interests and a full schedule. She even sounded happy. It must have taken a lot of work for her to move on the way she had.

Although the steak was excellent and he'd been starving, the more she talked, the more nervous he became. No way she wouldn't ask about what brought him to Alamogordo, and he wasn't going to lie. It didn't matter that his life had taken a sharp curve downward; the conversation would naturally lead to them both thinking about how Danny had run out of luck three years ago. That Sam had some nerve to complain at all.

His hunger abated along with his courage. He could have used some advice from someone wiser, more experienced. The way he and John had dealt with the aftermath of Danny's death was to not talk about it. They'd both been offered counseling and had passed. Sam was under no delusions that he had hidden behind his testosterone like a kid hides under the covers to keep the monsters away. He hoped like hell Emma had done more.

Maybe she was right to want to keep her distance. If they saw each other again, even once more, the elephant in the room would have to be acknowledged. But dammit, he did want to see her again. Tomorrow wouldn't be too soon.

"You all right?" Emma asked. Sam had been looking at her for a long while, which wouldn't have been quite as bad if she understood what was behind his furrowed brow.

He jerked his head back, pasted on a smile. "Yeah, sorry. I just…"

"Got lost?"

He nodded, then turned his attention to his meal. He cut a piece of meat, but instead of eating it, he reached for his wine.

"Is it too much?" she asked. "I understand if I bring back too many memories. Honest."

"What? No. I like seeing you. I was afraid I was making you uncomfortable. Jeez, no. You're the best part of coming to Alamogordo."

Emma blinked at that. *She was the best part?* That had to be an exaggeration. He was going to fly the Raptor. That was the brass ring for a guy like Sam. She'd caught him off guard, that was all. "Now that you're going to be living here, you can call it Alamo. It makes things a lot easier, and people won't think you're a tourist."

"Good to know. Thanks." With troubled eyes, he searched her face. "Look, I want you to know that I don't ever want to be a source of discomfort or make waves in your life. You say the word, and I might send you a Christmas card but that'll be it."

"No," she said, more vehemently than she'd meant to. "I mean, no, it's fine. It's good that you're here. I loved those years we were all a team. Those are some of my best memories ever. It's nice to be reminded of the fun parts, of how happy we were, even when there was so much pressure at school and then being transferred and everything was scary. You were…are a great friend, Sam."

He didn't respond right away. They even had time to order coffee. When he put his hand on top of hers, it was all she could do not to out-and-out gasp. Like the hug, his touch reverberated, expanding as it filled her chest. For whatever reason, the reaction was ridiculously disproportionate to the gesture. If it wouldn't have hurt his feelings, she'd have pulled free.

"I'm glad," he said. "I think about Danny a lot. But I think about you, too. John and I were talking about the four of us a few weeks ago. He sends his regards. I'm hoping he and his new girlfriend will come out here. We're not all that far from Vegas."

"Girlfriend? Guess it was bound to happen."

Sam moved his hand away, poured them each a few fingers of wine, which emptied the bottle. "Her name's Cassie and she's a psychology student who tends bar at her brother's place."

"Huh."

"I know." Sam grinned, and she liked that feeling of sharing a secret again. "He was surprised, too. I guess we all thought he'd end up with someone a little more…like his mom. I mean, as an air force wife."

"So it's serious."

"Who knows in the end, but yeah. It's certainly different. He's pretty crazy about her."

"I'm glad. He's a good guy. He's at Nellis, then?"

Sam nodded. "Test pilot."

Emma smiled, even though her first thought was about the danger of flying new aircraft. "Wow," she said. "That's fantastic. Scary, but great."

"But first, he's back in training. You know how that goes."

Coffee came, and Emma stirred in a half packet of sweetener. "Well, look at you two. Both of you in the desert, both of you having your dreams come true. I know Danny would be so pleased. He always said you guys were the cream of the crop. That you two were his only competition for hottest stud pilot in the U.S. Air Force. Guess he was right."

She lifted her cup, but halfway to her mouth she caught the look on Sam's face. Instead of the smug grin she'd expected to find, his expression had gone flat. Not even a hint of a smile curved his lips, and his eyes seemed shadowed as he stared down at his own coffee. It couldn't be because she'd mentioned Danny. "Sam?"

"I'm not here to fly Raptors," he said in a low, empty voice.

"I don't understand. That's all the 49th flies."

He looked at her and it was as if she'd imagined the past few seconds. His eyes were bright, his smile genuine. "Yeah, well, I've been grounded."

"You've…what?"

"I'm not flying. I, uh, had some complications from corrective eye surgery. I don't meet the requirements anymore."

"Oh, Sam." She felt his disappointment all the way to her soul. He could put on a show all he wanted but she knew what being grounded meant to someone like him… to any pilot, but this was Sam and her heart ached for him. "I am so, so sorry."

He shrugged. Sipped his coffee, didn't lose his carefree air. "I'm not out on my ass, so that's good. I'm an instructor now. For the MQ-9 drone. Which is cool because that's the future, you know? It's all about precision targeting and minimizing civilian casualties. I'm all over that." He chuckled. "We're in the same profession now. You'll have to give me some pointers."

She had no idea what to say to him. No amount of bright eyes or happy smiles would convince her that Sam "Jaws" Brody was anything but devastated at losing his wings. He lived for flying, just as Danny had.

God, the only thing that had gotten her through Danny's death was that he'd died doing something he loved more than breathing. More than her. "It seems so unfair."

"We both know how that works," he said quietly, and she lowered her gaze to her cup, hating that she was only making it worse with thoughtless remarks. "I'm okay. I was disappointed, sure, but I'm contributing. Hell, these men and women need instructors who are used to combat conditions. They deserve the best, and, well…" He spread his arms as he leaned back in his chair. "I'm going to do my damnedest to be just that."

She laughed with him, wondering how strong that facade of his was. What it had taken for him to make some kind of peace with this drastic turn of fate.

Thank goodness she'd agreed to the dinner. That she'd encouraged him to pick up their friendship. But she'd have to be awfully careful about their proximity, and her stupid reactions. Sam was a warrior to the bone, but he was also vulnerable. What he needed was a real friend. She'd leaned on him when her world had fallen apart, at least for a while, and now, she could return the favor. As long as she kept her own weakness in check.

Lifting her cup for a toast, she gave him the air force motto. "Aim high."

"Fly, fight, win," he responded, although his voice might have broken a bit on that first word.

3

"I'LL TAKE IT," Sam said.

The real estate agent, Mrs. Laurens, blinked in surprise. "There's more to choose from. The next one on my list is a great town house with a fireplace. I know that might not seem appealing now, but in the winter it can be very nice."

She had a point. This one-bedroom apartment was the first he'd looked at, and was probably meant to encourage him to increase his price range. But the place was clean, situated in the back of the property, so the noise wouldn't be bad. The grounds appeared to be well maintained, the furniture inside was about as nice as he could expect, so no sweat. It didn't compare to the Texas duplex, but it was fine. Mostly, he just didn't care enough to keep looking, so why waste the day? It wasn't as if he had anything else to do.

His things, including his Mustang, would arrive tomorrow, and he had no intention of staying in that motel one day longer than he had to. The horrible bed, the lack of coffee and the terrible TV were fine for a night or two, but after that it felt too much like a prison cell.

"Thanks, but this'll do."

The Realtor eyed the nick on the edge of the Formica

counter. "The place is nice enough, I suppose, but frankly, you can do so much better."

Sam hid his amusement. So she had been trying to jack up his price range. "How soon do you think I'll be able to get the keys?"

"The agency already preapproved you. There shouldn't be any reason not to get the key this afternoon." She frowned. "You're sure, now? The lease is for a year."

He glanced at the semifurnished living room. The couch looked relatively new, the overstuffed chair clean. The walls were painted white with no decoration, not even a garage sale landscape. Even the television was a bargain-basement brand with questionable color, but at least the place came with cable. The apartment might not be the best, but it wasn't the motel, and maybe he could fill some time here. Changing out the shower head was first on his list.

He honestly couldn't imagine Emma on that couch or chair. Which was another good reason to sign the lease.

"Would you like to come back to my office while we wait?"

"No, I'm fine. I'll go grab some lunch. Just let me know when I can get the key."

With an air of defeat, she shook his hand. "I hope you enjoy living in Alamo," she said. "It may be hot, but it's a good community. My husband is a civilian at Holloman, and he loves it there."

"I'm sure I will." He followed her back out to the front of the complex. When they reached the main parking lot he asked, "How far is the closest diner?"

She leaned to her left and looked past his shoulder. "Two blocks that way."

"Great," he said. "Thanks." He waited to hear the click of her car locks releasing and held the driver's door open for her. She didn't linger, for which he was grateful. Nice woman, but damn, he did not want to chat. While getting the apartment helped divert his attention away from Emma, it also made his new assignment a lot less theoretical.

In a matter of days he'd be in his classroom teaching both pilots who had transferred from manned aircraft and those who'd signed up for the short course, bypassing the long training and flight experience for immediate assignment as RPA pilots and sensor managers.

For the pilots like Sam, it would be a whole different ball game. The physicality of flying was a hard thing to remove from the equation. For those who'd done the undergrad training in Colorado and Randolph, this would be the ultimate test where they would learn the real tricks to maneuvering an aircraft remotely thousands of miles away, and what it would be like to be responsible for so many lives.

Sam would learn about himself, as well. He'd had limited exposure as a teacher, and nothing on this scale. It would be a real challenge. But it wouldn't be flying.

As he walked, the thought of never climbing into a fighter jet again overwhelmed him. In the year since he'd been grounded, these waves of doubt and anger still caught him off guard. In self-defense he switched gears. To Emma, of course. He'd almost called her a dozen times since dinner last night. He wasn't sorry he'd told her about losing his flight status. She'd taken it well. Said the right things. She wasn't a pilot, though, so she couldn't understand. Even all her years with Danny didn't help her get it. It was one of those things that you had to experience.

He almost passed the diner, he was so caught up in his thoughts. The place seemed okay. The health notice out front gave it an A grade, it wasn't a chain and only had two other customers.

The booth in the back had his name on it, and he settled in. A waitress, the only one he saw in the whole joint, gave him a menu. He ordered an iced tea, and that was it. He should have picked up a newspaper. A paperback. Something. He pulled out his cell, metaphorical fingers crossed, and sure enough, he was able to connect to the free Wi-Fi. Not a bad connection, either. But instead of clicking on the *New York Times* website or any of his favorites— Ah, who was he kidding, instead of calling Emma he ended up calling John.

"Jaws Brody, how the hell are you?"

Despite his mood, Sam couldn't help his grin. "Someone sounds like he's getting it regular."

"Someone is. Quite happily. How you doing, Sammy? You in Alamogordo yet?"

"Yep. I'm here. Looks like I've found a place to live, and it's hotter than hell here."

"You wanna talk hot? Come to Vegas, my man. In fact, seriously. You're on leave. Come out here. Meet Cassie. She's got friends. I've got friends. We'll set you up, you can have a nice time, then you can start your new life knowing what happened in Vegas will only be gossiped about among your acquaintances from Nellis to Kandahar."

"You make it sound so appealing."

"Hey. It'll be some laughs."

"I laugh plenty." Sam gave the menu a look but quickly realized he was going to order a burger and fries no matter what. "So I saw Emma."

"No kidding?" John's voice had gone back to regular, thank God. "How is she?"

"She looks great. She's teaching at the community college out here. The school's on the base."

"Wow. That's convenient. I think."

"Hold on a sec." The waitress had returned and Sam ordered, so he was back to the conversation in seconds. "She seems content. Involved. She's doing something with a local festival that I didn't quite catch, and she's on a bowling league."

The laugh was more of a quick bark that was so loud, Sam had to pull the cell away from his ear. "Bowling, huh? Does that mean she's with someone?"

"What? How does bowling mean she's dating? Anyway, no. Whether it's a lull between boyfriends or if she hasn't seen anyone since Danny, I have no idea."

"I wonder. You gonna see her again?"

"I think so. Yeah. I'd like to. I don't know who's stationed here yet. Haven't really been to the base. So she's promised to give me the nickel tour."

"I'm glad you called her." John hesitated. "Even though she asked us to give her space, I always felt like I deserted her. And then I was deployed a couple months later..."

"We were in mourning, too, and I doubt she needed us around as reminders," Sam said, but he knew exactly what John meant. "We did what she asked, and it was the right thing." He cleared his throat.

"You and Cassie, huh?"

John paused, and wherever he was, it was quiet. No jets in the background. "It's better than I imagined it could be, Sam. Looks like I'm gonna be flying the next-gen F-35, hot off the line. Training's good. The instructors know their shit. And going home to Cassie is the icing on the cake. I'd hate to jinx myself, but I gotta say, this beats the hell out of barhopping. No more of those awkward after-sex negotiations. And she's busy with bartending and school, so she doesn't mind my crazy hours."

Instead of hanging up like he wanted to, Sam forced a

smile, knowing it would show in his tone. "You lucky dog. It sounds like you've got life by the balls."

John laughed again, quieter this time. "I am lucky," he said.

"You deserve it. So don't screw it up."

"It's got nothing to do with deserving it," John said, surprisingly vehement. "If that was a factor the world would be a whole different rodeo. I'm lucky. I know it. I'm grateful."

"Me, too, buddy," Sam said, feeling the lie churn in his guts. "I'm gonna go check out my new classroom soon. Get the lay of the land."

"Good. I meant it about visiting, though, so give it some thought."

"I will. Hey, that was fast. My burger's here, amigo."

"Let me know how it's going."

"Right. Say hey to your lady for me."

"And you say hey to Emma."

Sam hung up, putting his cell on the table. His food hadn't arrived, just his tea. He drank some and tried not to regret the phone call. He was happy for John, dammit. But his jealousy was like a time-release acid tablet working its way through his system.

John did deserve the life he had. He'd worked hard to get there. He'd gone the extra mile when most people would have just said the hell with it. But so had Danny. And so had Sam.

Danny's accident had been a fluke. Sam was just one of the 10 percent you read about on the medical release form. Neither were *deserved*. By all rights, he should be strapping on a Raptor instead of standing in front of a chalkboard.

He finished off the tea and leaned his head back, closing his eyes. Emma. He had no business thinking about her all the time, but he couldn't stop. He'd thought about her long into the night, and she'd been his first thought this morning. As he'd signed up at the real estate agency, he'd written her name as a reference before replacing it with the manager of his last duplex. What had forced him out of the motel in the first place had been his shower. He had no business picturing her beautiful face, replaying the sound of her laugh as he'd let his mind's eye move down from her face, to the water cascading over her shoulders and breasts....

His food arrived. Eating, for all its benefits, was lousy at distraction.

Emma was his friend, nothing more. She'd be nice if he called, sweet as she showed him around town. That was who she was, but anything that happened from this point on would be more about old times' sake than starting something. She had her own life now, a full one.

She might not be seeing anyone at the moment, but there could be lots of reasons for that. Emma probably couldn't find anyone who could compete with what she'd had with Danny. Sure, he'd hung out with the guys a lot, sometimes too much, and there were a couple things about Danny that Sam wished he didn't know. But every time he'd been with Danny and Emma they'd been magnetic together. Polarized, as if being apart was against their very nature. The last thing she needed was a constant reminder of what she'd lost.

He took another bite, checked out a customer sitting at the counter. Dude looked beat-up in his wrinkled suit. Probably a salesman.

Sam sighed and downed some fries. He didn't dare consider pursuing Emma as more than a friend. That could only end in humiliation. Why would she want an instructor when she could have her pick of some of the best fighter pilots in the world?

Shoving his unfinished meal away, he decided to go work out. At least he'd be accomplishing something as he drove himself nuts.

HER CLOTHES were in the dryer and her web-class replies finished. Finally, Emma could sit down, have a cold drink, maybe even try to catch up on one of the shows that had piled up on her DVR. Her last task for the night, besides putting away her laundry, was patching up a boned corset for Sharon's play, and she could watch and sew at the same time.

Fresh lemonade poured, she took another look at her bullet list tacked on her fridge right next to her grocery list. Yep, the rest of the night was hers, although sadly she only had about an hour or so to enjoy it. Because her life was a thrill a minute, she tried to get to bed at eleven. Even though she didn't have early classes every day, after her long bout of insomnia she did her best to stay on a consistent sleep schedule. It worked most of the time.

She settled on the couch, sewing kit open, remote in hand as she went down the long list of things she'd meant to see. Television had always been problematic. She loved it like crazy, but she never had time. Before the advent of the DVR, aka the Devil's Video Recorder, if she missed something her disappointment had an end date. Now she could feel deprived and/or guilty for ages.

There was quite a backlog of procedurals, and as she clicked on a *CSI,* she thought about Sam, and how he could never watch any of the iterations without getting flustered about the absurdity of lab techs marching into active crime scenes, guns blazing. It didn't matter that it was fiction, or that most watchers apparently didn't care. He got riled up each time. And the guys consistently made fun of him for it. She'd done the same.

He'd been a good sport, though. Of the three, Sam was the most laid-back. If one could ever call a fighter pilot that.

She scrolled to a National Geographic special and pressed Play. Still her thoughts went straight back to Sam. Heck, everything since last night's dinner somehow ended up reminding her of Sam. Embarrassingly, she'd spent far too long pondering how stupidly good-looking he was. She'd met her share of average-looking pilots, but the ratio was such that she wondered if there was some psychological basis for handsome men to want to become pilots in the first place. There had to be.

The job itself was fraught with danger, took a lot of brain power as well as mechanical skill and was automatically assigned a heroic value. It was the perfect occupation for the archetypal warrior, imbuing the individual with characteristics they might or might not have in another context. In fact, she'd used the fighter pilot as an example in her creative writing class.

The thing was, the pilots she knew somehow managed to live up to the epic standards. They passed most of life's tests with soaring marks, with some notable exceptions. Few were destined for long-term commitments. Not to anything but their jets.

Which meant that no matter what he said or how manfully he smiled, Sam had to be utterly devastated by being grounded. It broke her heart, and the urge to do something about it was strong, but that was a slippery slope.

She threaded her needle and began to work, listening to the soothing voice of the British narrator talking about clouds. Five minutes in her cell rang.

Her pulse jerked into fourth gear until she saw it was

Gary. He didn't call often. Probably something about running. She thought about letting the call go to voice mail, but that seemed silly. "Hey," she said.

"Got a minute?"

"Sure. What's going on?"

"You know how I'm involved with Habitat for Humanity, right?"

"Yes," Emma said slowly.

"We're moving forward on a new home for a returning vet. We're past the planning stages, so pretty soon we'll be building the actual house. It's not a huge commitment, just whatever you can offer, but the people are nice, and I was thinking you might like to join me at the next meeting. It's Saturday afternoon. I thought we could go to dinner after?"

"Yeah, you've mentioned volunteering a couple of times," she said, knowing she didn't have anything for Saturday except the usual, and yet… "You know, this Saturday isn't going to work for me. I've got some things going on. But maybe another time?"

"Yeah, of course. It was a shot in the dark. Another time would be great."

"Just so you know, I can't imagine I'm going to be much of an asset in the building department."

"There are lots of ways to help," he said, his voice rising. It was so unlike Sam's deep rumble. "Writing press releases, for example."

Dammit. Enough about Sam already. "Thanks for thinking of me."

"I do," he said. "Think of you."

That stopped her. Until she laughed. As awkwardly as humanly possible. "That's…nice."

Gary cleared his throat. "Yeah, well. I should let you go. See you in the morning?"

"You betcha," she said. Which was even more awkward.

She clicked off as quickly as she could and stared at her phone as if the whole conversation had been its fault. What the hell was that all about? She liked Gary. Two months ago, when they'd started running together, they'd had their odd moments, but that hadn't lasted more than a couple of weeks. Maybe it was the surprise.

Or maybe it was her fixation on a certain pilot.

Dammit.

The buzzer on the dryer went off, and she disentangled herself from her sewing. But on her way to the laundry she got sidetracked by the big wooden bookcase against the far wall. Not the case per se, but the photo album that stuck out two inches farther than the rest of the books in the row.

It was in her hand a second later and before she knew it she was back on the couch, legs curled under her, fingers hovering over the goofy front photo of her and Danny on a sailboat. They looked so young.

She opened the book for the first time in years. Her favorite wedding photo stole her breath but surprisingly didn't make her feel as though a hot fist was squeezing her heart.

What a babe he'd been. She hadn't been so bad herself. They'd had a ridiculous, slapdash Reno quickie marriage at the tail end of a raucous weekend of skydiving and gambling. None of her family had been there. Just Sam and John. They were the witnesses, and instead of throwing the confetti they'd bought from the chapel as she and Danny had made their way down the steps, they had poured the cursed teeny pieces of paper straight over their heads. They kept finding stray remnants all through dinner and the celebration at the nightclub. In the end, she and Danny had dealt with the problem sensibly by trading up to a Jacuzzi room and letting the whirling water save the day.

She flipped the page, then the next. In the beginning, there'd been several solo pictures of her or Danny, but the guys showed up more and more frequently. Camping, studying, skiing and snowboarding, out for drinks, dancing. So many good times. Then the time between pictures stretched. And stretched.

She stopped at a photograph of the four of them; she had no idea who'd taken it. They were at a restaurant; she remembered the champagne they'd had with that dinner to mark the occasion. The boys had just completed their JSUPT, Joint Specialized Undergraduate Pilot Training, and had received their silver wings.

Everyone but Sam had smiled hugely for the camera. Sam, meanwhile, had kept his gaze on her.

How had she not seen it? The longing in his face spoke volumes. They'd always had that certain something, but when the boys had gotten their wings, things between her and Sam had changed.

This was not good. Sam and she, they had too much of a past, too much history for a casual friendship. She wasn't interested in pilots. A year ago, she'd decided to try dating again. Scared to pieces, she'd met a guy at a karaoke bar. She'd agreed to a date, and when he'd come to pick her up, she discovered he was air force. Not a fighter jock but a cargo pilot, so there was some distinction. Though not enough. He was good-looking and dangerous and funny and smart. Everything she'd found fantastic about Danny. They didn't make it to the second date. Her fault, not his. She refused to be one of those women who kept being drawn to the wrong man over and over again.

Then she'd tried dating again two months later. He was everything Danny wasn't: a corporate attorney, a real fan of old black-and-white films, divorced, no kids. She'd been bored to death.

Gary was a perfect blend of the two. Smart, funny, nice-looking. But safe. Safe as houses. He owned his home, liked to bowl, got along with everyone, and his last relationship had ended when his live-in girlfriend had gotten a job in Asia. The breakup had been friendly.

So why had she put him off about Habitat for Humanity?

She looked down at Sam's face.

Sam was a good man, but underneath his laid-back ways there was a need for danger. He never risked anyone else's safety, but he was a man who liked to live on the edge. Danny and John and Sam, they'd been on everyone's list of bad boys at the Academy, and they'd earned their reputations. Though Danny and John more so than Sam.

Sighing, she laid her head back. If she was going to start downplaying Sam's past, that was reason enough for her to be cautious. He might be grounded, but he wasn't put out of commission. She had no idea what he would do to replace that singular rush of flying an F-16, but it wasn't going to be a sudden passion for bowling.

If she had any sense at all, she'd keep her distance. Be polite, have a meal with him, preferably lunch at the base, from time to time. Talk about the good old days.

But she couldn't help thinking that he didn't have Danny or John around to help him make the biggest transition a pilot could face. As far as she knew, he had no friends at all at Holloman.

Whatever else, he'd been an incredible friend to her and Danny. He was alone and hurting. There couldn't be any harm in helping him get settled. She'd learned her lesson with Danny. Dangerous men weren't just dangerous in the sky. She wouldn't let herself make that mistake again.

4

"Emma. Hi. How are you?" Sam winced at his complete failure to sound casual. The day had been a bitch, and the desire to call her had been overwhelming. That she'd taken the initiative made everything better.

"I'm good," she said, with all the aplomb of someone who wasn't nuts like him. "Just wondering if you'd gotten your car yet. Or if you'd been able to look for an apartment. I've thought of some nice places since we had dinner. I can email you a list."

He paced the length of the living room, avoiding boxes and the crappy TV he'd replaced with his own fifty-inch LED. "Thanks, but I've got it covered. I found an apartment yesterday, got my things delivered today."

"Wow, so quickly? You must have checked out apartments at a dead run."

"Naw, it wasn't a big deal. I liked the first one and if I know one thing, it's how to facilitate the paperwork." He'd ended up in the kitchen without remembering walking there. Opening the fridge, he reached in for a beer. "In fact, I've already been to the base and finished all the transfer crap."

"Wait a minute. You took the first apartment you saw? Is it at the Versailles complex?"

"Nope, this one's called something else. El something something."

"Oh. Why so hasty? I thought you have a lot of leave."

"I do. But why keep looking if this one fills all my requirements, including an attached garage? Can't have the Mustang living on the street."

"Okay."

The single word was filled with skepticism. He didn't mind. She was just being Emma. He wanted to ask her to come over. Right now. Even though the place was a mess, and he wasn't much better. Talking to her would have to do, though, because he'd made a commitment not to push. Not on the phone or in person.

The last thing she needed was to put up with him whining and moping because he couldn't fly anymore. That was his own damn fault. He'd known there were risks to the eye surgery, but with his arrogant bulletproof attitude he'd dismissed the possibility with barely a thought.

"How was it at the base?"

"Fine. I wasn't there long. Just enough to make sure my paycheck's sent to the right address."

"What about your classroom? Is it what you expected?"

Sam was pacing again, and he reached the far side of the living room in no time. "I didn't make it there. I was expecting the moving van, so I figured I'd wait to explore the base until I was more settled."

"That…makes sense." She paused "Hey, how would you like some help with that? I've got a free day tomorrow and I could come over early. Are you allowed to paint the walls? You know how good I am at that. Or I can line the kitchen shelves and all the drawers and cabinets. We could maybe have lunch or something. It'll be fun."

Her rapid-fire speech made his shoulder muscles relax better than any massage. This was the old Emma, and it was like hearing a favorite song from back in the day. She was always the one who organized everything. Vacations, parties, moving. Hell, she alphabetized her books and her spice rack. They used to call her Monica when she went all commanding officer on them. Like the character from *Friends* who was a neat freak. "You're a lifesaver, but I'm gonna have to go to the BX and buy a bed first. The one here stinks."

"Let me come out and take a look at the place…you probably need things. We'll make a list, then I'll go with you."

She sounded like a kid on Christmas. He wasn't about to argue. He didn't give a damn about lining shelves, but seeing Emma again? He couldn't think of anything better.

ARMED WITH BAGELS and two kinds of cream cheese, Emma felt her heart sink the closer she got to Sam's new apartment. It wasn't as if the complex was a pit, it was just… not Sam.

He was the kind of guy that wouldn't give a thought to what someone else drove, or how they dressed. But he had a fighter pilot's ego, and he'd always presented himself as a confident man of style. Every time he'd moved it had been to a place that mirrored that mind-set.

This was the kind of place that you took because you couldn't afford better. And he could.

She'd meant the call last night to be friendly. More a polite inquiry than anything else, with a vague promise to meet for lunch in the future.

The moment he'd said he'd taken the first apartment he'd seen, she'd realized something was wrong. She shouldn't have been surprised. He'd lost flying. Of course he was going to be upset. Depressed. Knowing he might be in trouble made it impossible to stay away.

They were friends. Time hadn't changed that. She could do this. After a deep breath, she knocked on his door.

The moment she saw him, the rush she'd had at the restaurant hit her again. Hard. She wanted to blame it on his cologne, but he didn't use any, or his clothes, but he was wearing worn jeans and a T-shirt that had seen better days. The smile, though, the one that was like sunlight, that was a big part of it. The rest was an alchemy she didn't understand. Couldn't afford to even think about. It would pass.

He leaned forward as if to hug her, but stopped himself as she took a step to her right. She giggled, he winced, then they did the same dance but in reverse. The bagel bag came to the rescue when she shoved it in his hands and swept past him into a living room that sent her mood plummeting. If she'd thought the outside was bad...

White walls, not even a good white. Beige carpeting that would have fit into any medium-priced motel. The furniture was nondescript and the whole place lifeless.

Boxes were piled against the long living room wall, along with a television and an open toolbox. At least he'd done something since moving in. Although he might have fixed up his bedroom and bath.

"Would you like some coffee?"

She turned. "Sure. Did you look in the bag?"

He shook his head and waited for her to lead him into the kitchen. It was as dull as the rest of the house. White appliances, Formica countertops, linoleum flooring. And small. Which, to be honest, wasn't a big deal for Sam. He wasn't big on cooking, unless he was grilling.

"That has to be yours," she said, nodding toward the fancy one-cup coffee brewer.

"That, the TV and my laptop are the only things I can't

live without, and I could probably manage without the laptop."

"A person needs to have priorities," she said, opening a cupboard. There was a large supply of coffee pods and a box of Pop-Tarts. Nothing else.

"Breakfast of champions," he said, reaching over her shoulder for a couple of pods.

Unsettled by his proximity, she slid over to the fridge, almost afraid to see what he'd stocked in it.

"Go ahead and open it. I know you're dying to."

Emma gave him a mock glare, even though he was right. The corners of his mouth lifted, making her insides flutter, and she quickly returned her attention to the fridge. Beer. Yellow mustard. A pint of milk. "So, you need a trip to the commissary, as well."

"I suppose I do." He was washing out one of the cups that had come with the apartment. It was awful, and small. His travel mug, which was a respectable size if not elegant, was sitting on the counter next to a bag of fast-food wrappings and used napkins.

"Are there any mugs hiding in those boxes?"

His hands stopped. "One. But I'm not sure which box."

"No problem. Maybe while we're at the BX we can pick up a few. In case you have company." She went over to put a mitigating hand on his shoulder, but stopped herself just before she touched him. "Those are horrible."

"I know." He shrugged. "Maybe I should box up all this kitchen stuff and replace it, but that's just one more thing to move when I get transferred."

"Do you think you will be? So soon?"

He finished with the washing, and set to brewing, and wow, it smelled great. "It's the military. I always expect to be transferred."

"I sure don't miss that part," Emma said before she'd

given the remark any consideration. Though she was considering it plenty after Sam's sharp look. One she couldn't quite read, but it wasn't hard to guess it was about Danny. "Want to give me a tour while the coffee brews?"

"Oh, it's not going to take that long," he said with a laugh that seemed to make everything right again.

The rooms were large, which was a plus, just blah. The bedroom set looked as if it had been bought at a motel auction, the bathroom lighting was a nightmare, and even worse, he'd put his whole wardrobe away in the hanging moving boxes.

"That does not look like a comfy bed."

"Hey, it's not so bad. At least the lumps in the mattress distracted me from the missing support slat in the frame. I'd let you see for yourself, but I like you too much."

She laughed and he grinned, and for an instant they were back in Colorado, where they'd first met, before life started throwing curveballs.

THEY'D FINALLY MADE IT to the bedding section at the BX. It was his first trip here, but God bless the air force for making every base exchange basically interchangeable. There were a few fast-food places that hadn't been in Texas, and the better restaurants were different, but he felt more at home here than he had since he'd arrived.

Emma had been busy on the way. It seemed as if she'd picked up at least one thing from each aisle, sometimes a lot more. Plants had been something of a surprise. Not that she'd picked up some, but how many she'd chosen. Half his morning would be spent watering the suckers. And then there was the fountain. He had no desire to listen to the soft trickle of water as he went about his day. But she seemed to think it was the best thing since sliced bread, and into the cart it had gone.

He didn't care. Really he didn't. She was in full-on Monica mode, and that was the best thing ever. If he had his way, they'd spend all day here, him with his hands in his pockets, her going over her list and telling him the whys and wherefores of her purchases. He couldn't wait to get her to the office supply area. There was no doubt in his mind she would want to organize him within an inch of his life. And he would happily let her.

"Inner spring mattress?"

The way she asked the question made him look up from the big display model. "I had one at my duplex. It was good."

"Have you ever tried memory foam?"

"Can't say I have."

"You should try both. I'm madly in love with my memory foam. It's like it was custom-made for me."

"Really?"

Her enthusiasm was a sight to behold. Her brown eyes sparkled, she spoke quickly, as if she couldn't take a chance that something might interrupt. "It's amazing. Truly. But try an inner spring first, because any bed you try now is going to feel like heaven after that nightmare in your apartment."

"Good point." He wasn't crazy about lying down in the middle of the huge store, and if the purchase wasn't such an important one…it was the first major piece of furniture he'd be carting from base to base…he'd never have done it. But he did.

She was right about the mattress feeling awesome. He'd read that you were supposed to try out a bed the way you actually slept, and since he was a side sleeper, he did. It was awkward, because now he couldn't help watching strangers walk by. Most of them were in civilian clothes, but within the first few minutes, he saw three pilots. They didn't have to be in uniform for him to know. They wore the job one hundred percent of the time.

He turned over, away from Emma and the view beyond her. This time he closed his eyes, though, and concentrated on the feel beneath him.

"Okay," he said, as he sat up a minute later. This one felt like the one back home, and he was tempted to just buy the damn thing. "Which one next?"

Emma was all too happy to be his guide. On the third mattress, he shook his head. "It feels just like the other two."

"No, it doesn't. This one has individually wrapped coils, and the last one had continuous coils."

He sighed, really not getting the difference. "Okay, let's start at the beginning, and you test it, too."

Never one to turn away from a challenge, she went straight back to number one. She was already in place, her head on the pillow as she rested on her side, by the time he got there. He joined her on the bed, and they were eye to eye, and close enough to touch.

"Oh," she said, blinking. "You meant test it together."

He froze, not sure what the hell to do. "I don't know what I meant."

Emma laughed. "Okay, well, we're here." She pressed down on the mattress between them and started talking about offset coils. Like a dog with a bone, she wouldn't stop until she got her point across.

That was bound to take a while, since he couldn't stop thinking about how much better this would be if the mattress was set up in his apartment. If there was no piped-in music or dozens of strangers milling about. If it was just him and Emma all alone in the bed…

He had no business staring at her like this. Not when

she was so tempting. When he could count her eyelashes, and lose himself in the sound of her voice.

"I see you two have narrowed down your choice," a man said from about a foot away. Sam nearly leaped off the bed and tackled him, he was so caught off guard. "It's a honey. Perfect for a young couple like you. This model has a great warranty, and you can get the same features, but with a dual firm selection."

Sam rolled off the mattress, and so did Emma. He hoped he wasn't blushing like she was.

"We're not a couple," she murmured. "We're just testing out different models."

"I was hoping to try out a memory foam next," Sam said, walking toward the other end of the display area.

"Absolutely, follow me," the salesman said, even though he had to practically run to catch up.

Sam felt like an idiot when he turned to find Emma pushing their very full cart to join them.

"Which one do you have?" Sam asked as he helped pull the cart close.

She took him to the third one from the end. "I think this comes extralong."

He just climbed on, not caring whether he liked it. He wanted to finish shopping, see if he could get the bed delivered today, or if he'd have to rent a trailer.

As he settled on his side, he realized she'd been right. It was a fantastic feeling, like the mattress was molding to his body, made to order.

"Don't rush it," she said. "Let it cradle you."

He looked up at her, her smile approving, her short hair in spiky tendrils that seemed to frame her face so she glowed. He wanted her so badly. Had wanted her for so long. It wasn't just the new assignment. Not transference or any of that psychological bull. This was the Emma he'd fallen for years ago. The Emma who didn't belong to him. Never had. Never would.

He rolled over to his other side, cursing his reckless thoughts. He'd better get it together, and damn fast, because if he couldn't then he'd have to make some excuse to send her on her way, and that would hurt like hell. She was the one bright spot in his life right now, but he could only keep her in it if he kept his distance.

It took him longer than it should have to calm down, but it was okay, because she was pleased he was taking her advice to heart.

When he finally got up, he told the salesman he could write up the order. Emma made sure every *T* was crossed while he called the apartment complex and made sure the maintenance guys were available to help him move the old bed out and the new one in.

There were still aisles to explore, and even he'd underestimated the amount of time a person, or at least Emma, could spend looking at containers. And buying containers. "What's that one for?" he asked, staring at a very similar piece already in the cart.

"Your multiuse drawer."

"You mean the junk drawer."

"If you think of it like that, then it will get filled with junk. The organizer is to help make it easy to find your miscellaneous items."

"Uh-huh," he said, absolutely sure he'd end up with a junk drawer, only one with less flexibility.

"You wait and see. You'll thank me in the end."

He grinned at her and rested his hand on her shoulder. She was so slender and delicate it made him feel ridiculously protective. "I'm thanking you right now. You've been amazing. I never would have thought to measure so much stuff before we left, or to go through the boxes I had shipped so we wouldn't duplicate efforts."

Her smile was surprisingly shy. "I am pretty good at this stuff."

"Pretty good?" he said, removing his hand before he was tempted to run it down her back. "You should have your own organizing show."

"I have been offered money to help people get their stuff together."

"You didn't take them up on it?"

She shook her head. "I only do this for people I know well. Without understanding the human element, organizing a house can go FUBAR really fast."

"And you know me really well."

"'Course I do. For example, I know you're going to just throw stuff into the multiuse drawer for about three months, until you can't find something important, then you'll give in, and it'll make your life easier."

"Three months, huh?"

"Give or take."

Christ, he wanted to kiss her. If she wasn't Danny's wife...if Sam were still flying... "I'm sold," he said, moving back to take charge of the cart. To clear his head he stared at the amazing number of items he was going to be buying today. Things for his walls, his counters, his drawers, his cupboards. Not only was this day costing him a fortune, he had no idea where most of this stuff was going to fit.

"I know what you're thinking," she said, and when he glanced up she was staring at their epic load.

"Yeah?" he said, grateful that she also realized they'd gone overboard.

She nodded somberly then looked up at him. "We're going to need a second cart."

5

IT WAS TWO before the perishables had been put away, the old bed had been replaced by the new, and all the shelves in the kitchen had been lined. Emma should have been in her groove, thinking three steps ahead, making sure that neither of them was wasting time. Instead, she was going over those few moments of being in bed with Sam. And how, at least before her brain had kicked into gear, it had felt like the most natural thing in the world. In fact, it had felt *right*.

She put the remaining roll of shelf liner in the bucket she would take from room to room, the one with the cleaning supplies. She thought the shopping itself had gone really well. When they were finished, the apartment would have heart and vibrancy and would set the tone for his period of adjustment.

On the other hand, that brief stint in the middle of the store when she'd looked into his eyes had set her pulse racing so fast it still hadn't settled back to its natural rhythm. Since then, every time she saw him or heard his voice, the infamous spark flared. She felt like a pinball machine.

Behind her, Sam approached, still catching his breath

from moving mattresses. "You want something to eat?" he asked.

There it went again. How could he not see the way she jumped in her skin, the way her breath quickened? She wasn't hungry, but that was probably because she'd been doing the fight-or-flight adrenaline shuffle most of the morning. But she should eat. He should, too. They weren't nearly finished putting things away.

She raised her gaze and met him with all the cool she could muster. "How about a quick sandwich?"

"Sounds good," he said. "Depending on how we do this afternoon, we can kick back tonight with a pizza and some of that merlot we picked up." Thankfully, he turned his attention to the meat compartment in the fridge. "Ham and cheese? Turkey? Bologna?"

"Turkey please. Light on the mayo, heavy on the sprouts."

"You got it."

She hummed a bit as she put the dishes in the cupboard. Maybe a song would help keep her occupied so she could stop obsessing. Not so easy when sharing this tiny kitchen with Sam. She could go start on the living room, but that made her eye twitch. All the hard work, the rinsing and lining, was finished, so the rest should be a snap if she didn't weaken.

But he moved, he breathed, he cleared his throat, and everything else faded into a blur. Something had to give, and okay, if she couldn't completely beat him, perhaps the trick was to include him. "Do you still eat those fluffer-nutter things?"

The mayo container landed on the counter with a bang. "Oh, man. Why'd you have to say that? I don't have anything but the peanut butter and I don't want to go out again."

"So that's a yes?"

"It's been ages," he said. "But now I want one like crazy."

"White bread, Marshmallow Fluff and peanut butter? That isn't a legitimate food item, let alone something a grown-up would eat. I'm surprised someone hasn't made a law banning them."

"You wound me, Emma. You and your whole grains and your kale. Need help with those platters?"

She almost said no, but they belonged on the top shelf, which was a stretch. Sam stored the platters and she couldn't help but notice his trim waist as he did so. And his ass. The man had a world-class backside. All the other waitresses at the Rusty Nail, where she'd worked a lifetime ago, had voted him best butt at the Academy. Even her loyalty to Danny hadn't let her disagree.

Using every bit of discipline she had, she aborted her moan along with the urge to touch.

EMMA HAD QUICKLY AVERTED her gaze, even as she flushed pink and pretty high on her cheeks. She shooed him away, and he wondered if it was because she was as worried about this thing between them as he was. "We're almost done in here," she said. "After you finish eating, we'll tackle the living room, okay? You have to install the DVD player and set up the sound system, right?"

"Um, mind if I make our sandwiches first?"

"What?" She didn't seem anxious to meet his gaze and waved a hand. "Oh. Right. No, go ahead."

"Thank you."

She turned sharply toward him, her eyes narrowed. "Are you laughing at me?"

"No, ma'am. I don't want to have to finish unpacking by myself."

Emma couldn't seem to hold back her grin. "That's a distinct possibility, so watch it."

"She boldly says to the man in charge of making her sandwich."

Immediately she stopped putting away utensils to watch him spread a light film of mayo on her whole wheat.

"Don't worry," he said. "I know exactly how you like it."

"How on earth do you remember that?"

"Are you kidding? The way you chewed me out the time I spread mayo too close to the crust?"

"I was never that picky."

He lifted a brow at her, and she gave him an indignant sniff, then turned back to what she was doing. But he knew she was keeping an eye on how much turkey he measured out for her.

"When I'm finished here," she said, "I'll start putting away your LPs."

"You know they—"

"Go in a certain order." She gave him an indulgent, very Emma smile that twisted him up inside. The way they knew things about each other made everything harder.

Honest to God, he couldn't decide if the deep pleasure of being with her was worth it or not. It was like eating a whole package of Oreo cookies. So good while they were going down, and nothing but regret after.

It wasn't just seeing her that had him wishing he could freeze time. Knowing she was going so far out of her way to be there for him was downright intoxicating. Yeah, he'd let her get a little nuts at the BX, but he knew she was determined to make this place feel like a home instead of a prison. Unfortunately, every moment spent was another memory sure to torment him.

Whatever else he was, Sam was not naive about what was happening here. Their history was against them, and their future had no chance. That left casual friends.

No way. No way he could pull that off without going insane.

Dammit, he didn't want to lose her. Not after just finding her. Knowing she lived in the same town, worked on the same base, was going to be as difficult as listening to the jets he couldn't fly take off and land every day.

Why on earth had he signed up for another ten years? Maybe there was a way to get out, some kind of mental health clause that would still leave him a shred of dignity.

She turned, surprised he hadn't finished making their sandwiches yet. "Everything okay?"

He nodded, went back to work. He thought about telling her to leave, that he appreciated what she'd done. He wouldn't, though. He wasn't strong enough for that. No, he'd savor every second he had with her, try not to make things uncomfortable and let her go with great reluctance. What the hell, right? His fate had been sealed the minute he'd answered her call.

He put her sandwich on a napkin and then handed it to her. He didn't bother to ask if she wanted to quit working to eat since he already knew the answer. She'd only taken her second bite when he polished off his turkey and Swiss. Man, he'd been hungry. He wouldn't make a second one, though. He would get back to work so they could relax with that bottle of wine later. Just the thought got a reaction from his body. Sad. Very sad.

Standing in the middle of his ugly living room, he looked at the opened boxes, at the bags from the BX. He should be used to moving by now. He'd done it so often, but this time…this time was the worst. Probably because there was nothing to look forward to. "Hey, remember that house John and I rented in Texas?" he said, watching her over the counter that separated the two spaces.

"I do," she said as she put the dishcloth down, then

checked each of the newly stocked cupboards. "I remember how you screamed like a little girl the first time you saw a flying cockroach."

"Nice," he said as he lifted the box that held the tabletop fountain she'd bought. "Very nice. I was going to mention that great mural you made for us, and how terrific it looked, but now I'm not going to."

"Ah, that's sweet. It was good, though, wasn't it?"

He snorted at her, wondering whether she'd just replace the fountain if he slipped and dropped it. It probably wouldn't even break landing on the carpet. Throwing it against the wall would work.

Her laughter got louder as she joined him in the living room. She'd obviously already figured out where to put the albums because she went straight to a pot shelf that looked as if it would hold his whole collection. And the stereo system would fit well on the broad ledge that ran next to it. He had to do some thinking about where he'd put his speakers, though.

Emma was on the floor, cross-legged, and he got stuck, staring. He'd been thinking a lot about her hair. What it would feel like between his fingers. Soft, he'd bet. Soft as her skin. His gaze moved to her knees. It was hot outside. Would have been nice if she'd worn a sundress or a pair of shorts or something. But he could picture what was under those jeans. He'd seen her plenty of times in her bathing suit, in cutoffs. One time, he'd caught her wearing one of Danny's shirts, unbuttoned halfway and barely covering pink panties.

Not on purpose. It had been over in a flash with a high-pitched squeal and a dash back to her bedroom. But he'd remembered her thighs. The flat plane of her tummy. Then he'd felt like shit for having those kinds of feelings for his best friend's wife.

He went to work on the stereo, keeping his eyes forward, focused. He heard her as she shuffled the records, the distinctive swish of cardboard against cardboard. It didn't take him long. He could have done it blindfolded. But then he got the stepladder he'd borrowed from maintenance and used special adhesive hooks to hang all four wireless speakers around the room.

He finished before she did and plucked the record from her hand as she was about to put it away. He should have looked first. It was *Physical Graffiti*.

"'Kashmir,'" she said.

"Yeah," he said, quietly. Danny's favorite song from his favorite album. All Sam had wanted to do was test the sound levels.

She closed her eyes, and he thought about putting the album away, changing the subject, but when she looked up from her perch on the carpet she said, "Go ahead. Play it."

"You sure?"

Emma nodded as she turned back to the albums on the pot shelf. "You still keep the make-out music separated? Use them much?"

He put the vinyl on the turntable and when it started with "Houses of the Holy" the sound was pristine, as if he was playing it for the first time. "Not for a while," he said. "I seem to be the last of a dying breed. Most of my friends are married or with someone. I'm thinking John might be the next one to fall."

"You're against marriage?"

"No. I can see myself getting hitched someday. Having a couple of kids." He listened for a minute, wishing he could think of a slick way to change the subject. He tried to see if the speakers were balanced well, but his distraction levels were off the charts.

As he crossed over to the box that held the DVD player,

she said, "I can't believe we haven't discussed this before. Or am I just not remembering?"

"I don't think we ever did," he said. "Not seriously. You tried to fix me up so often that I figured you hated that I was single. I didn't want to encourage you."

"That wasn't meant to get you married. It was to help you have better taste in women. Jeez, you and John both needed someone to set you straight. After a while, the women became interchangeable. I never did understand that."

"It was for fun. We were highly motivated testosterone machines all during our twenties." What he couldn't tell her was that there was only one woman he'd cared all that much about, and she was taken. "Danny was the odd man out." His regret was instant. "No offense meant."

"Plenty taken, but do go on."

He smiled at how easy she made it. "You guys got hitched before he'd even finished the Academy. It was a radical move."

She turned to look at him. "Did you think it was a mistake?"

"No. No, God, we thought it was great. But you guys were young, and there was so much we all didn't know about our future. It was a tough road you chose. But in the end…"

"What?"

He sighed, wishing they were talking about anything other than Danny. "Turned out, you made him…better."

She stood, leaving the second box of albums untouched. "What do you mean?"

He couldn't look at her. So he fiddled with the inputs and outputs and the HD hookups. "The longer you were together, the more grounded he became. There were some things to worry about with him. He was prone to reckless behavior."

"More than you were?"

"Really?" He frowned at her, shocked to see that yeah, she seemed completely serious. "I was into danger sports, but I was pretty safety conscious. Okay, not always, but mostly. But Danny…he took some radical chances."

"Like…?"

"Illegal base jumping. Skiing in the backcountry, fresh slopes that could have had any kind of hazard under the powder. That kind of thing."

"I thought all three of you did that stuff."

"John and I tailed him for the most part. To make sure he didn't— Shit, Emma, I'm sorry. I don't think we should be talking about this—"

"It's okay," she said, and he had to look at her again, just to make sure that light tone wasn't feigned. "Danny's not a forbidden topic. I still think about him, just not as often. It's been three years, and I've finally gotten used to the idea that he's really dead. It took longer than I'd expected."

"It's hard when there's no reason. When there's no one to blame."

"Sometimes I feel guilty for not thinking of him more." She ducked her head. "Even though I've built my life around staying busy. I've got students I tutor, web-only classes, I help out with the drama department. I go running with a friend a couple of times a week."

"At Holloman?"

"Nope. At one of the local high schools. With a friend," she repeated as she walked past him to the kitchen, but she slowed her step before she hit the linoleum. "His name's Gary. He teaches mathematics at the college."

"Oh?" Sam's gut twisted. He shouldn't care. She was

free to see anyone she chose. In fact, he should be glad for her, but... "You said you weren't seeing anyone."

"I'm not. He's a colleague."

"Uh-huh."

"We've never been out on a date. We don't... It's not like that."

"But you're thinking about it?" he asked, then immediately cursed himself for being an idiot.

She sighed. "You want a beer?"

Sam nodded. *Yep, and maybe some duct tape for my big mouth.*

She disappeared into the kitchen and he heard the fridge open and close. A few seconds later her voice carried over the music. "Oh, for crying out loud," she said. "What the heck is this doing here?"

"Shit," he muttered, knowing exactly what she'd found. He should have put the stupid thing in the trunk of his car instead of trying to hide it. Moving into her line of sight, he said, "I was hoping you wouldn't see that."

She held the thing up. "It's a mug with boobs, Sam."

"It's nothing. Hey, it's not that bad, and I don't use it in mixed company."

"Why do you even have it?"

"It was a gift."

"From the boob fairy?"

"From Danny, actually. He got me one, and John one."

"Huh. I'm gonna go out on a limb here and guess that he bought one for himself, as well."

Sam nodded. "I think John has it."

"A mug with boobs, Sam. It's a mug. With boobs."

"I'm a terrible person. I know that," he said. "But, well, I'm gonna keep lugging that stupid thing around because it meant something to us."

"That you've never left puberty?"

He laughed, but he'd never been more glad to have that ridiculous mug. Now all he had to do was keep things light until after dinner.

"OKAY, IF WE DON'T STOP and eat soon, it won't be pretty."

Emma grinned. It was so good to hear the humor in Sam's voice, the ease with which they'd been working together had erased her earlier misgivings. "I gather you're hungry."

"You're not?"

"I could eat."

He dropped an empty box on the pile that had been accumulating since they got home. The living room was nearly finished, thankfully, although there were still things to be done in the bedroom and the bathroom. "Still like veggie pizza?"

She stopped fussing with the throw she'd picked up for the couch. "I know we said pizza, but would you be horribly offended if we had sandwiches again? I'd like to keep our momentum going. I can't stay all that late, so you'd better use me while you can."

His frown suggested he had his heart set on pizza, and she was about to give in when he shrugged. "You know what? Whatever you'd like is fine with me. But you need to promise me that I can take you out for a real dinner. Whenever it's convenient."

"You don't need to—"

He held up a hand. "I've kept you busy all day. I'd never have gotten this far without you."

"True, but it's also my fault that we're not done yet. If I hadn't cornered you into buying half the BX…"

"I have no regrets."

"Good. Then it's a plan. I'll take care of the sandwiches while you go make up your bed. Deal?"

"Deal. I think I'll go all out and have ham and cheese with mustard this time. That goes with merlot, right?"

She grinned on her way to the kitchen. "A match made in heaven."

Before he left, he turned over the Dave Grusin jazz album that had been their background music for the past half hour. Sam smiled at her as she passed. If she didn't know better, she'd have thought he looked a little melancholy, but that didn't make sense. They'd been talking away as they'd worked, and it had been almost like old times.

When he finally came back to the kitchen, she'd opened the wine to let it breathe—although she doubted ten minutes was going to do much—made three sandwiches, two for him, and had doled out some potato salad to go with it.

The atmosphere, when they both sat down on the floor by the coffee table, assured her that nothing was wrong. He scarfed like the starving man he was, and she wasn't exactly a dainty flower herself. They'd worked hard, but they'd accomplished a lot. She could already feel the difference in the vibe of the place. It would take some time to feel lived-in, but it was better than the institutional ward look that had alarmed her this morning.

When Sam went to pour her another half glass of wine, she stopped him. "I've got to drive home, but thanks."

He nodded, put the bottle down, but left it and their glasses as he cleared up the dishes and put them in the kitchen.

The last box in the living room was marked *pictures and files,* but given the state of some of his packing, she wouldn't count on it. But when she opened it, she saw a pile of loose photographs. A quick look below showed a few had frames, and below that was a stack of folders.

There wasn't time now, but maybe some day she'd bring over a couple of albums and put the mishmash in order.

The top picture was a very young Sam in a too-large protective suit, a muddy helmet and gloves, standing next to a motocross bike.

The next was a grainy picture of him with his mother. She looked harried but happy. Even though Sam was probably eleven or twelve, he looked like a miniature version of the man in front of her.

"What's next for me?"

"How about breaking down the boxes and putting them in the garage?"

She barely registered his nod, anxious to get back to sorting and straightening. And yes, she was enjoying the pictures, too. The next few had been taken at a park, but she didn't recognize anyone, and then began the photos of his Academy years. Danny and John were central players, of course, but he must not have taken a lot of pics between first and second year. Then she showed up. Some were different angles taken at the same time as some of her own collection. A couple she'd never seen before.

She stopped, though, when she uncovered a photograph of her. Just her. She knew where they had been and remembered the day. They'd been celebrating John's birthday. Emma hadn't realized Sam had taken the picture in her hand, but somehow it didn't surprise her. Not after she'd seen the stare that had been caught on film in her own album.

It must have been very uncomfortable for him. It certainly had been for her. And yet they'd both kept the snapshots.

She buried the portrait in the pile, and kept on going. Graduation, moving to Texas, getting their silver wings. Toward the bottom, just before the files, her breath caught as she saw a terrific five-by-seven of Sam in his flight suit, climbing down from the cockpit of his F-16. "Now, this is a great picture," she said.

The sudden silence after all the tearing of cardboard made her realize the music had stopped.

"What picture?"

She stood, taking the photo to him. "This is one you should definitely have framed."

Sam glanced down, and the way his smile vanished and his expression tightened instantly clued her into her mistake.

She lowered the picture. "I'm sorry. I shouldn't have—"

He gave her a look that wrenched her heart. The sadness in his eyes seemed to go all the way through him. "Forget it. It's fine."

Emma caught his arm as he started to turn back to the pile of boxes at his feet. "Don't," she said. "Please. I'm so sorry I brought it up, but you don't have to pretend. Not with me. I know what mourning is like, Sam."

"I'm not mourning," he said, but he fought against meeting her gaze. "I've had a year to adjust."

"I get it. I do." She moved closer to him, hoping he'd look at her. "The alarm used to ring and there would be a minute, sometimes two, where everything was great and I looked forward to the day, and then I'd remember, and it was like all the color got sucked out of the world."

He did look at her, but then, just as she saw a hint of moisture gathering, he closed his eyes, tight. The muscles on his arm bunched and locked, his body grew rigid as he struggled to keep himself contained.

Her hand moved to his nape as she took that last step that closed the distance between them. When she tugged him down to meet her in the middle, he struggled. But not for long.

6

SAM KNEW he should turn around, stop this before it got started. The brush of her lips alone was enough to shake him to the core. He'd wanted her for so long. But even as he started to move away, she pressed up, her lips parting, her wine-scented breath filling his senses.

She pulled him closer, and hearing her soft whimper, his surrender was complete. Knowing there would be hell to pay, he took what she offered, brushing the small space between her lips with his tongue. She opened for him and when they tasted each other it was almost more than he could bear.

Still holding his neck, her other hand swept up his back to his shoulder. Small, delicate, yet strong enough to grip him, to keep him right there.

It was impossible to stay still. He wrapped his arms around her, careful not to squeeze too tight. Not to expect too much. He'd never imagined he could have her like this. That he could know what it was like to feel her press against his body. Kissing her was better than any of his fantasies. Of course, he'd cut those short, never daring to go past a look and a touch when he was conscious. In his dreams, however…

Now he was desperate to feel everything he could before it all disappeared.

She jerked back, gasping for breath, and Sam panicked until she kissed him again.

The body pressing into him was small and firm and there were too many clothes. Even so, the feel of her back, the way her waist tapered only to swell with the curve of her hips, hit him hard. His imagination had kept her distant and cool, something to yearn for, never to hold.

Christ, his palm nearly covered her entire buttock. Of course he knew she was slender, petite. When he was younger, he'd pictured himself lifting her. Carrying her away from some vague danger, and she'd been light in his arms. But nothing compared to the reality of her small breasts rubbing against his chest. He couldn't be sure if he really felt the points of her hardened nipples or if his mind was thoughtfully filling in the details.

The urge to lift her now burned from the inside out. It about killed him to hold himself in check. But this was Emma and he had to be careful. He'd take whatever she wanted to give and nothing more. And he'd be damn grateful for it, too.

Their mutual panting grew suddenly loud, as if speakers had been turned up. Then her hand moved from his neck, her left leg shifted back. The kiss ended.

He might as well open his eyes. It didn't matter if they were red and betrayed his traitorous emotions, he needed to see her. To freeze the image of her swollen pink lips, the darkness of her pupils, the flush of blood as it swirled so close to the skin.

Her gaze held more compassion and understanding than he knew what to do with, but before he could run, her hand was in his, tugging as she took a step closer to the bedroom.

"Wait," he said, the word turning to ash on his tongue, but it had to be said. "Are you sure?" was all he managed, even though he meant, *Is this just pity?*

Her smile dimmed, but her eyes never left his. She didn't drop his hand, either. Instead, she studied him. Maybe her own motives, as well. "I'm sure. Are you?"

He couldn't have not kissed her then. Not for anything. Their lips met, hard and hungry, and he was still utterly amazed. But far too quickly, she was tugging him again, abandoning his mouth to hurry him forward.

He thanked everything that could be thanked that he'd made the bed. Of course, he had to tear it down again, but only so he could push back the covers.

Then he was in front of her, staring down at her face, memorizing her chin, her cheeks, her delicate little nose. She had thick eyelashes that curled up and a light smattering of freckles across her cheeks. Unable to resist, he touched her hair, feeling clumsy and oversize as he let her short tresses slip through his fingers.

"I think I'm going to start a little lower," she said, pausing, but if she was waiting for an argument from him, she wouldn't get one.

He only smiled, then felt her tug the bottom of his shirt from his pants. Once she had it free, she undid the top button and kept on going. Somewhere around his belly, he realized her hands were trembling.

He abandoned her hair, took her hands in his. "Are you okay?"

She nodded. "It's been a while," she said. "That's all."

"You sure? Say the word and we stop. No matter what."

Dragging him down to her lips, she whispered, "Shut up, shut up, shut up," until the kiss took over. Long and deep, both of them teasing and thrusting in a frenzy, he lifted her T-shirt up and away. Promising himself that he'd continue the kiss the second they were in bed.

She went back to unbuttoning his shirt and it didn't take long to finish. He let it drop where he stood, mesmerized by her sexy little bra. It was light green, and it did absolutely nothing to hide the hardness of her nipples.

He wanted to see her breasts bared, but he also wanted to see her in her underwear. Yeah, naked could wait a minute. His hands went for the button on her jeans, but all he managed to do was get in the way of her trying to do the same to him.

Their tussle sounded like a slap fight for a few seconds, but she stopped him with a growl. "I'll do mine, you do yours."

He grunted his assent, too busy toeing off his shoes and unzipping to form words.

He stopped breathing when her jeans dropped to the floor. Shit, she wore bikini panties, strings on the sides, the V like an arrow showing him the way. They were white. Perfectly plain, and devastatingly sexy.

His erection had reached critical mass, and he wanted more than anything to strip off his boxer briefs. Well, not quite. With one step, he was inches from her, and then he was on his knees. He leaned into her, his face pressed into the tender flesh of her belly. Inhaling her scent made his cock jump with nowhere to go.

Her hands touched his head. Closing his eyes, he breathed deeply as she petted him, the moment surreal and perfect. When he had gathered enough of his wits to move again, he went lower, catching the elastic of her panties and tugging them down. He felt more than saw her neatly trimmed hair, her scent getting stronger, so intoxicating he felt light-headed.

Inelegant and impatient, he gave up the slow tease and

used his hands to finish the job. Naked from the waist down, she spread her feet apart. He had to stop again, just stop.

He couldn't help it—his own situation was becoming increasingly uncomfortable. Burying his nose at the top of her mound, he quickly pushed down his cursed briefs, moaning as his erection bobbed against his stomach.

When he leaned back to get his bearings, he saw that her blond thatch was one shade darker than the hair on her head. She was impossibly beautiful. He wanted to kiss her until they were both breathless, but that would mean standing and he wasn't sure he could, even if he was willing to abandon the pleasure before him.

IT WAS ALL Emma could do not to pull Sam's hair. She was shaking as the heat of his breath got closer. And then, a kiss at the top of her sex. Chaste in its own sweet way. Which only made her tremble harder.

She wanted more. Everything, in fact. Just this time. Just this once. She wanted him to forget that he couldn't have his jets. For him to wipe her mind clean of anything to do with shoulds and shouldn'ts.

As if he'd heard her silent plea, he spread her open with his thumbs and chaste flew out the window. Her hands tightened in his short hair, her moan starting low but getting louder the second he focused the hard tip of that wicked tongue on the exact perfect spot.

Her head fell back and her eyes rolled as she let the waves of pleasure wash over her. This was it, the mindlessness she'd wanted for both of them. Time out of mind, out of thinking and worrying.

Turning grief into comfort, pain of the heart into bliss of the body.

His fingers were suddenly inside her, two of them, pushing up and in, and she bucked, couldn't help it. He followed her, never losing contact, and how were her legs holding her upright when all her bones were melting? "God, Sam. Please."

"What do you want?" he whispered, leaving his post.

It might not have been a delicate move to guide him back into place, but she didn't care. She could already feel the beginnings of an orgasm gathering like a storm deep inside. "This," she said, although the word turned into a hiss when he pushed and pressed in a way that made her give up all illusion of control.

Perhaps he understood that standing wouldn't be an option soon, because he sped everything up. Clenching his fingers wasn't a conscious choice, and oh, there. It began, and she rose up on straining legs, held her breath and gripped his shoulders as if he could save her.

Her body contracted on a pulse that shot from her toes all the way up. Sparklers lit the inside of her eyelids, and her mouth opened on a silent cry that reverberated in her chest.

She nearly screamed when he was suddenly standing, lifting her up onto the bed, next to her, over her. When his knees touched the inside of her thighs, she reacted in slow motion, spreading then bracing her heels on the mattress.

A sharp curse made her open her eyes. Blinking, she watched him lean over the side of the bed. His thick erection bobbed underneath him, his foreskin retracted completely, the head glistening with his want of her.

As he came back, a condom packet held like a trophy in his upraised hand, she lifted her hips, telling him to hurry. He got the message.

One last yank of a pillow from the head of the bed to under her butt, and then he straddled her, his biceps bulging when he braced his hands on either side of her shoulders.

He lowered his head just as she raised her own, and they kissed. Deeply, and for longer than she thought possible. The man had patience and fortitude, she'd give him that. Finally, it was she who broke away. "Now," she said, her voice a scratchy mess. "Please."

"God, yes," he said, using one hand to guide himself into position.

He looked into her eyes before he pressed in. His pupils were huge, his breath frantic. She stared openmouthed as he filled her. As his eyes squeezed shut and his lips peeled back revealing his gritted teeth.

She almost contracted around him, but held off. He was clearly using all his self-restraint to resist, and not just come with the first thrust.

It wasn't easy for her, either. Her body had its own agenda, which she had to fight. The only thing to do was close her own eyes, use her hands for something that wouldn't make him crazy, if that were possible.

She ran her palms up steely arms, then gently over the plane of his back. She hummed at the feel of his warm skin, at being this close to him. "It's all right," she said, looking once more at his face. It could have been pain and not desire written in his closed eyes and in the grimace of his mouth. Maybe it was. Maybe they were destined to feel both at the same time. She'd lost Danny and all the dreams that she'd placed in him, and Sam had lost his planes, and the rosy picture he'd painted of his future.

Maybe this moment was meant to remind them that there was still joy to be wrung from tragedy.

She watched his face relax in stages. Caught the second he figured out that it was okay to move. The first new thrust was slow and deep. The second made her gasp.

His gaze on her face was as penetrating as his cock pushing inside her; she held on for all she was worth, unable to look away or speak. The thought that she might be hurting him was gone in a flash. Then he moved in, lifting her legs so they wrapped around his hips, and he was rubbing against her again, not as narrowly as with his tongue, but who the hell cared when it was sending her out of her mind.

His moaning made her open her eyes, and only then did she realize she'd shut them again. He was still staring at her, but the moan was her name. Her name, over and over again. Emma, Emma, Emma, and that was all it took.

She arched up, gripping the linens now, and she was coming. Hard, God, it was like earthquakes and lightning.

He froze, and all she could see were the tendons straining in his neck, the flush spreading from his chest, the tight groan trapped behind pressed lips. They stayed that way for a few endless seconds, her letting herself savor her release, him looking at her as if he'd been waiting for this moment his entire life.

It was a scary thought, and probably entirely off base.

She dropped her legs, and he fell to his back, gasping loudly. Or maybe that was her. It didn't matter. She couldn't think anymore, or move, or catch her breath. Not while the aftershocks kept rolling through.

The next thing she knew, there were blankets and warmth, and she turned to press herself against his body. His arm pulled her closer, and she muttered his name, but couldn't stay awake long enough to see if he'd heard.

HE WOKE TO THE SCENT of Emma. Before he opened his eyes, he accepted each inhale as a gift, a mix of sex and her. Just…her.

That this was all a dream was very likely. He'd had a number of them over the years. But none of them had been so detailed.

All he had to do was look down, see if he was truly holding her as she lay against his side. He could even feel the pressure of her head on his chest, her arm around his waist, and yes, her leg halfway over his thigh.

No, this had to be real. He opened his eyes, unprepared for the rush that coursed through him. The jolt was similar to how he felt taking off in an F-16, to the moment he punched through the clouds. All right here with Emma curled into him. Nothing had ever come this close to flying before. It probably should've scared the hell out of him. Not made him smile.

A shaft of sunlight sneaking between the blinds shone like a spotlight on her face. While he liked seeing her in such amazing detail, he carefully edged his shoulder up so that she wouldn't wake to that kind of intrusion. Now she looked softer. Very tousled. Damn, but he finally knew what her hair felt like. For real.

It had been real. He'd been in pain, and she'd come to him. Her beautiful face concerned and caring. He remembered the first touch of her lips more clearly than his first solo flight. It had felt impossible. So long out of his reach that he'd trained himself not to believe it could ever happen.

Tempted as he was to run his hand down her arm, he held off. He needed the time to adjust to this new world. A world where it wasn't all self-restraint and wishing for something that could never be his.

She was here. In his arms. And they'd made love.

Actually, he'd have thought this would be weirder. That guilt would have taken over and left him broken, but instead, he felt peaceful. As if this was meant to happen.

Danny had been gone awhile, and maybe, if he could see, he'd be pleased that Emma was taken care of now. Sam wasn't one for superstition of any kind, and he hadn't believed in the afterlife since he was a teenager. Oddly, that didn't matter. Because it all made sense now. His transfer to Alamogordo, of all the bases in the world. That Emma would still be here three years after Danny's accident. *Destiny?* He had no idea. Whatever it was that brought the two of them together, he wasn't about to complain.

Damn if he didn't think this might have a real shot at working. Him and Emma. They were already friends, so there was that. And now it was clear they were compatible in the bedroom.

She moved her hand, and then her head, and Sam froze. He wasn't sure if he wanted her to stay asleep longer, or wanted to revel in her waking up in his arms.

He let it happen naturally, and what a sight. Her nose scrunched up for a second before she tucked her face right in the crook of his shoulder. When she straightened her leg, it caught him off guard, but he didn't jerk too hard.

There was a muffled something, not really a word, and then her hand went to her head and she turned once more, face up, eyes opening once, twice. He thought she might yawn, but it stopped with a clench of her jaw.

She seemed to get her bearings a bit at a time, as well. When she finally looked up at him, she smiled, and yeah, it was the best thing ever.

"Morning."

She sniffed. "Morning. What time is it?"

"Don't know. The clock's behind me. I think."

Emma lifted her head, but then the sun hit her square in the eye and she let herself drop. "I suppose it doesn't matter."

"Right. It's Sunday. No work."

She nodded. "Sorry I crashed so hard. I guess all the work of the day caught up with me."

"I followed right after. No problem."

She shifted against him and it finally registered how very naked they both were. He'd love to go again, but he had the feeling that it might be better to wait. Given what he remembered about her and mornings, she'd probably appreciate caffeine first. At least he hoped that was what the brief but awkward silence was about.

"Hey." He gave her a hug, kissed her forehead and then, as much as it pained him, moved over to give her space. "I've got a cup of coffee with your name on it coming right up."

She rose up on her elbows, the sheet covering her breasts, squinting, even though his body still blocked the sunlight.

"You'll have to settle for regular sugar this time," he said, not bothering to locate his jeans. "But I'll pick up the dark honey you like for next time."

Something shifted. One second to the next, and his heart stopped. It was in her eyes, in the wince she tried to hide. And there, when she ducked her head and looked away.

What had he done? God, he'd just taken the ball and run the full nine yards with it. And he hadn't even been close.

"Thanks," she said, still not looking at him. "But since I've been running in the mornings, I have coffee after."

"Right. Of course you do." He was off the bed before she could say anything else. He was a moron, a stupid fool for jumping the gun, for thinking for a minute that everything would suddenly come his way.

She'd felt sorry for him. That was all.

He pulled on a pair of boxers as quickly as he ever had, cursing to himself because he was half-hard and she had to have seen it. Before running out of the room, he picked up her clothes, put them on the bed. The little green bra underneath her T-shirt. "I have an extra toothbrush," he said. "I'll put it on the bathroom counter. It'll only be a minute."

"Wait." Her hand touched his arm, and he almost jerked it away. "Sam, please. You don't have to rush. It's all right. I know it's a bit awkward now, but last night was really special for me. I hope it was for you, too."

He cooled his damn jets. Just because he'd been an idiot didn't mean he had to be a dick. She'd been kind. And he'd be thankful. He would. Any minute now. "Of course it was. You're amazing."

"I'm your friend." She grabbed her panties and slid them on while she was still under the covers. After a moment's hesitation, she got up, turned around and put on her bra.

He closed his eyes until he heard the sound of denim sliding up her legs.

When she faced him again, it was with a hesitant smile. "I know more than anyone what it's like to lose the most important thing in your life." She touched him again, and it was all he could do to stay calm. "I couldn't stand you being in so much pain."

He nodded. Now it seemed so obvious. She'd been carried away by the moment. That was all.

"Your friendship means the world to me. I just got you here, and I don't want to mess that up. I hope I haven't made a mistake."

"No," he said, and there was a part of him, the part that wasn't bleeding, that was telling her the truth. "You didn't. We're fine. Honestly. I'm so glad you were here yesterday. And last night." He leaned forward and kissed her on the cheek. "Sure you don't want to sneak in a cup of coffee for the road?"

"No, thanks. I want to get home. Shower. But tell you what, let's have lunch this week, okay? Maybe on the base, or I could take you somewhere you might not have tried."

"I owe you, not the other way around. The house looks great."

She frowned as she slipped into her sandals. "We're not done yet."

"I've got it covered. I already stole too much of your weekend. Let me go get that toothbrush."

He headed straight for the bathroom, opened the package he'd stored under the sink and left her the pink brush. He didn't look in the mirror at all.

7

EMMA HALTED three steps into the faculty lounge. It was the second time that day she'd forgotten what she'd come in there for. Dammit. It was all Sam's fault.

He hadn't called her since Sunday morning, and now it was Wednesday, and she hadn't stopped thinking about him for five minutes. Okay, that was a slight exaggeration, and it technically wasn't his fault that she couldn't get him off her mind, but it felt better to blame him nonetheless.

Because if she didn't blame him, she'd have to blame herself, and who was she kidding, she knew that what had happened was totally on her. She'd had one job. *One.* Don't get romantically involved with Sam. The past seventy-two hours was a prime example of why that rule had been put in place.

Pure instinct had driven her to offer comfort. She'd seen his pain, and it had been so achingly familiar she couldn't have done anything else. That her response had been so physical was only slightly surprising. Their mutual attraction had been simmering for ages, but even with all that history she'd never imagined that sleeping with him would be the most…what? Fantastic sex she'd had in years? Confusing thing in the world? Unintentionally brilliant move she'd ever made? Or all of the above?

She knew the right answer. What to do with the jumble that was her mind was another problem altogether.

After pulling out her chilled lunch bag, she closed the fridge, but didn't head back to her office. It was that third option that stopped her. Unintentionally brilliant? She'd had bits and pieces of thoughts heading down that road, but she'd cut them short. What would it even look like if that wasn't a one-shot deal? If she and Sam became lovers?

The shiver that went through her was an indication of her body's vote, but her body wasn't always a reliable source. She'd made the decision not to get involved with Sam based on a past that couldn't be ignored.

Aside from everything else, Sam didn't even know the real truth about her and Danny. Once he did, this debate would most likely be over.

So, not brilliant. Although maybe not a disaster, either. What if she just put everything on hold? Waited until she talked to him, explained about Danny first, and then, later, how she wouldn't even entertain the notion of being with Sam if he'd still been flying.

Would he understand? She wanted to think so, but he hadn't called her since Sunday, and what did that say? Maybe he was fully invested in the two of them remaining friends. The last thing he needed was to enter into a tricky relationship when his whole world had been turned upside down.

She winced at the image of his face when she'd showed him that picture. She could count on having that stupid move come back to haunt her for years to come. What had she been thinking?

Although it had led to spectacular sex, and good grief, her knees felt wobbly as she remembered the way he'd touched her. How his kisses had left her breathless, and how much she wanted to wake up in his arms again. Only next time, she wanted to stay for coffee and have her own toothbrush.

Pausing to get her mail, she remembered to pull her cell out of her purse. She hadn't turned it on, since she'd had back-to-back classes and office hours in between. There were two voice mails. The first she immediately ignored because the second one was from Sam.

"Emma, hi. I wanted to thank you again for all you did to help me move in. Of course you left me not only with a deskful of really interesting-looking containers and no idea how to use them, but more important... While I appreciate the idea of a fountain, and the theory that trickling water sounds are relaxing, all it's done so far is make me want to pee ten times a day. So we'll see.... Anyway, thanks again. Uh, thanks."

Her grin had begun at the sound of his voice. By the third word, the butterflies had started fluttering so hard she'd pressed her lunch bag to her tummy. The fountain bit made her laugh, and even his awkward ending was totally endearing.

She replayed the message, and had the exact same reaction, only more so.

"Well, at least we know she's not in a fugue state."

At the sound of Sharon's voice, Emma spun around. She hadn't even realized. Her friend was sitting at a table not ten feet away, and Gary was right next to her. Esme Trajillo, the ESL teacher, was also in attendance, her lunch salad almost finished. "How long have you guys been here?"

"Since you walked in looking like a zombie," Sharon said. "At least until you listened to that call. Who brought you out of your trance?"

Emma busied herself with putting her cell back in her purse so her friends wouldn't see her heating cheeks. "Just an old friend."

"Does this friend know how to bowl? Because Carla can't make it and we were already down to bare bones. I don't want to be out of the championships because we don't have a full team."

"We're two and seven, Sharon," Gary said. "I don't think we have to be too worried about the championships."

"I always worry," Sharon said, returning her attention to her sandwich. "It's my natural state."

Ignoring her, Gary turned to Emma. "Joining us?"

"Can't today. I've got a class I'm not ready for after lunch, then I have a tutorial. But I'll see you in the morning, okay?"

"You bet," he said. "You sure you're all right?"

Emma wondered what he meant, but couldn't make anything out of his expression. "Yeah, I'm fine."

"Good," he said. "Tomorrow."

She nodded, still puzzled, and headed for her office. She hadn't been completely honest with them. She did have a class and a tutorial, but she was prepared for both. What she intended was to return Sam's call.

First thing she'd do—ask him to come bowling. It was a perfect way for them to see each other again. Neutral territory, plenty of folks around. It was fun, too, so it might lift his spirits. Besides, he needed to make more friends now that he was stationed here.

It bothered her a little that he hadn't brought up the dinner he owed her. Not that she cared about the meal itself, but rather that it wasn't like him not to mention it. The most important thing to her was that no matter what, the two of them remained friends. Whether or not there was more to it than that, well… Dammit, why was she even going there? Before she saw him again, she'd better be real clear that being friends was it for them.

She had to shift over in the hallway to get past a gaggle of young women who were all gathered around one particular girl, someone Emma didn't recognize, on a cell phone. Clearly speaking with a boy. The girl was doing the hair-fling, the blushing, the grinning and the nervous shuffle, the traditional mating call of young love.

It wasn't until Emma had almost reached her door that it hit her why Gary had been concerned about her. While she hadn't played with her hair, she was guilty of all the rest. *Oh, crap.* She and Gary had been moving along so nicely, too. Sure, it had been slow as molasses, but she'd liked it that way, and had even been responsible for the slower pace. In fact, bowling had set their friendship in motion. It had been on one of their league nights that they'd decided to run together. Yet she still wasn't sure she wanted the relationship to go anywhere.

Obviously. She hadn't slept with Gary after a couple of months but she'd slept with Sam the second time she'd seen him.

Groaning to herself, she shut the door behind her and put her lunch bag on her desk. She took her cell phone out once more and simply stared at it. Would bringing Sam to the lanes while Gary was there be a problem? She doubted it. Nothing happened at bowling except bad shoes and the occasional gutter ball.

God, she hoped she wasn't being foolish. It was bound to be harder to see the charm of Gary with Sam around. He was so much more…more.

She sat down, not even a bit hungry, and pressed Sam's number before she lost her nerve. The flutters began before the first ring, and by the time he answered, she'd completed the quartet of mating rites by twirling a lock of her hair around her finger.

"Sam. How would you like to go bowling tomorrow night?" she asked with exactly no preamble. "Remember I told you about needing a ringer? We're a man down, and we could use your help."

"Uh—"

"And, it'll be fun."

"In that case, I don't see why not. This is an amateur league, right? I think I warned you that I bowl about as well as I dance, and I don't dance."

"You'll fit right in, I promise."

His chuckle made her blush as she rolled her chair back to the credenza. God, she could be the poster girl for adolescent crushes. Which was ridiculous. She'd known Sam far too long to be acting this way.

"You got my message?"

"Yep, and don't ditch the fountain yet. You'll get used to it."

"You know this for a fact?"

"Yes. Maybe. I'm pretty sure."

"Can't argue with that," he said, his tone dry as a bone.

She giggled. Giggled! "If you hate it in another week, we can renegotiate."

"I suppose I can make it through another week. While I'm thinking about it, I won't need to keep score at this bowling thing will I?"

"No. We have a mathematician who takes care of that. I mean our team does. We don't hire mathematicians for everyone."

He laughed, she smiled, and it felt pretty darn good until she started wondering about seeing him for the first time since…that…in front of all her friends. Maybe it would be better to get that part over with. In public, of course, so she wouldn't do anything stupid.

That she even had to worry about being a dope was troublesome enough. "You know, I'm here on the base, and I was thinking about grabbing some lunch. Are you in the area?"

"Oh, no. I'm not," he said. "I'm at a bike showroom across town, taking a look at a Hayabusa."

"What is that, a mountain bicycle?"

"Ah, nope. It's one hell of a motorcycle. Named for the Japanese peregrine falcon."

Emma's heart plummeted as Sam's voice rose in excitement. *A motorcycle.* The one thing she and Danny had argued about more than any other. More than money, more than him going out with his fellow pilots. He wanted one of those sleek racing bikes so badly he'd tried to win her over time and time again. She'd been adamant. The way he drove a car made her crazy. The way all the hotshot pilots drove bordered on suicidal, and she'd had nightmares about him spinning out on a bike.

Wow. She'd certainly gotten carried away. Sam, who was going on about engine size and Brembo something brakes, was a pilot, through and through. Whether he was in a cockpit or in a classroom, he was still a fighter jock, a man who lived for speed.

What was wrong with her that she continued to be so attracted to men with a death wish? Sam and Danny were cut from the same cloth; she'd always known that. That need for speed was one of the things that had almost done them in before the accident. What Sam didn't know, what no one knew, was that she'd been planning to ask Danny for a divorce. She simply hadn't been able to handle coming in a distant second.

There was a good reason she and Sam could be nothing more than friends. No matter how great the sex had been, or how much she liked him. Having her heart shattered once was enough.

"Emma?"

"It sounds great," she said, not even caring if her response matched the conversation.

"Yeah, I'm still gonna look around some more, though. Can't make a decision like this on a whim."

"No, you can't," she said, hoping he meant it. "I've got to get going, but I'll text you the address of the bowling alley, although there is only one in town."

"See you tomorrow night," he said.

She hung up and rolled her way back to her desk. No more hair twirling for her. Which was probably for the best. They should be friends. Casual friends. The trouble was, if anything happened to him, it would still hurt like hell.

WEARING HIS SHORT-SLEEVED uniform again after being in civvies felt good, like home. Or as close to home as possible now that he was living in an alternate universe.

He wasn't going to think about anything but the meeting he was about to attend…. Nope. Not yet. As he made his way from the Suzuki dealership to the base, he couldn't help thinking about Emma.

The call this morning had been difficult to make. He'd struggled with himself for most of two days, but finally gave it up as a no-win situation. It all boiled down to a simple choice: life with Emma or life without her. It was a no-brainer. He'd even try not to regret their night together. The ache it left behind wouldn't be easing anytime soon. Keeping busy helped. The bike would help, too, if he decided to buy it. With the modifications he wanted it would cost him a bundle, but since he hadn't shelled out a lot on a place to live it would balance out.

He looked around, not sure he remembered this street on the way to the dealership. Ah, there was a Chinese place that he'd noticed. Emma loved Chinese food, especially moo shoo pork. He should have asked her to dinner before bowling.

Bowling. There would be people there, her friends. Teachers probably, and there would be introductions. He'd be asked what he did, and it was difficult to imagine saying anything but *pilot*. He could say he was, and he wouldn't be lying, but unless he ever got back in the cockpit, it would feel dishonest. He was an instructor. He'd get used to it.

At least Emma would be there to ease the way. She understood what his change of status meant to him, and he was pretty sure, after that faux pas about the picture the other day, that she'd handle the situation with grace.

God, he couldn't wait to see her.

There was a school he recognized. And a couple of fast-food joints he'd stopped by. The base was getting closer, and he'd better focus on the meeting.

He wasn't back on duty yet, but he would've been unhappy to miss this informal session with the other drone instructors. The program was still relatively new, unlike manned flight training. The biggest hurdle he'd face would be treating all his trainees as equals, whether they'd gotten their pilot's license two years ago or flown fighter jets for ten years. His personal feelings had no place in his mission, and he would be damned if he let it influence him in any way.

But Sam also needed to adjust to his fellow instructors. They were all pilots, of course, but he'd wager most of them had come to Holloman because they wanted to be there. It would be interesting to read their attitudes as he gathered his first impressions. It didn't help that the F-22 Raptors were also on the same base and that there was no place to hide from the sound of those engines.

Five minutes later he passed through the gates, then drove out to the RPA training ground, an auditorium that would hold the three-hundred-plus members of this class, classrooms that would hold approximately twenty trainees at a time, and most important, a collection of sand-colored trailers that were spread out near the runway and maintenance hangars. In the distance were the jagged hills that reminded Sam of the terrain of Afghanistan.

There was a parking lot reserved for instructors, but he was early, and there were only a few cars parked. The heat of the desert hit him when he started walking toward the hangar where the meeting would be held.

He saw Colonel Ed Stevens, the man responsible for Sam coming to Alamo as a drone instructor. With him were a major and two other captains, and they looked exactly like a group of pilots hanging out by their F-16s. No one here was going to look down on him because he wasn't flying.

What he didn't know but was sure to learn quickly was how the Raptor pilots and the Reaper instructors and pilots got along. Probably mixed as little as possible, if his own history was anything to go by.

He saluted his senior officers and introduced himself to those he hadn't met. The welcome was warm but the bona fide questions started immediately. What had he flown, where, who'd been his commanding officers, and did he know this pilot or that instructor? The spotlight moved to the next new guy, who turned out to be a new female instructor, a cargo pilot late of Wright-Patt. She was given the same grilling, and by then, the full complement of instructors had arrived, and Colonel Stevens took the controls.

Halfway through the speech, Sam knew that this life would eventually become his life, that he'd make friends, discover his strengths and weaknesses as an instructor. Make mistakes, do the right thing, give his all. He'd tackle the challenges as they came up, and he hoped that in the end he'd be proud of his service.

But the sounds of fighter jets taking off was a dirge, a constant reminder that if he hadn't been a vain, arrogant idiot and just dealt with the glasses and contact lenses, he'd still be where he truly belonged.

8

SHE'D BEEN BOWLING for over a year now, and Emma hadn't been this nervous her first night, when it would have been a miracle if she'd hit even one pin.

Now she had her own ball, shoes and shirt. Her team was called the Three Rs, and they had three English teachers, two math teachers and one engineering teacher, who'd signed up late. Tonight, Carla was with her sister, who was having a baby, so Sam would take her place. Carla was a lovely woman—Emma liked her a lot—but she was a crap bowler. The team wouldn't be the same without her, though, because she told the most spectacularly dirty and hysterical jokes.

Emma slid her bowling ball case under the bench seat and kept staring at the door. Other teams' members were arriving in dribs and drabs, and she waved and chatted a little. They were all teachers from UNM-A so it was nice and friendly.

A lot of spouses came, too. Just for fun. After they bowled the three games that counted for the league, a lot of folks went to the lounge and hung out playing pool or darts. She usually went home.

Sharon was standing near the bar, talking to Leo, and

she, too, was wearing her embroidered Three Rs retro bowling shirt. They were dark blue, had their individual names emblazoned over the pockets, and a cartoon logo on the back. She didn't have a shirt for Sam, but that was okay. He probably would've hated wearing one, anyway. No. She allowed herself a small smile, knowing he would've flat-out refused.

She couldn't stand it, and went into the ladies' room for a few minutes. Sam was due, and she was still reeling from their phone conversation yesterday. After she'd hung up, she'd looked up the motorcycle he'd talked about on Google, and it was exactly what she'd feared. The top speed was over a hundred and eighty miles per hour, which was insane right there. That should have been all the information she'd needed: that Sam was considering buying one told her everything.

But she couldn't let go of last Saturday night. She should have known it wouldn't be that simple. The urge to talk him out of his recklessness had messed with her since yesterday. It was a fool's errand. The bike was only a symptom, and even if he did eventually agree with her, he'd end up doing something else equally dangerous.

The need for speed. It was a joke among pilots, but it was no laughing matter. She'd known pilots who weren't in the least rush-hungry. Not the way Danny, John and Sam were. The weird thing was, they were the most careful of pilots in their fighter jets. Seriously, they were all about safety first. It was just that flying Mach 2 wasn't enough.

She thought back to what Sam had told her about Danny being the most reckless of the three of them. She wondered if that was true, though he'd had no reason to lie to her. And in fact, he'd obviously regretted bringing up the subject. No use giving the matter any further consideration. Sam wanted that insane bike. That was all she needed to know.

She fluffed her hair out, ran her hands down her recently ironed shirt and went out to the lanes again. Sharon was already in her shoes, hands on her hips and a glare in her eyes. "Why'd you run off like that?"

"I went to the bathroom, where did you think?"

"You could have at least said hello. I gather your friend isn't here yet?"

"Nope, but he should be arriving any minute."

"Who, your pal?"

Emma turned at Gary's voice. He'd come from the direction of the desk, carrying their score sheets. "Yeah. He's never late to things. Oh, there he is now."

They all faced the door. Poor Quentin, who'd come in just ahead of Sam, thought the rousing welcome was for him, and he seemed so pleased, she and Sharon both waved.

Sam looked around until he spotted her, then smiled. It was like being stuck by an arrow, straight to the heart. What the hell had she done to herself?

"This is your old friend?" Sharon asked. "He's gorgeous."

"He was a friend of my late husband's," Emma said, wishing Sharon had left out the commentary in front of Gary. "They went to the Academy together.

"Another pilot," Gary murmured, his brows furrowed. "He must be happy to be assigned to the Raptor."

"He is a pilot," Emma said, walking to the rows of bowling balls against the wall where she met Sam as he came down the three stairs. "Any trouble finding the place?"

"The huge Bowl-O-Rama sign made it reasonably easy. Should I go get shoes first?"

"No, come on and meet the rest of the team." She almost reached out for his hand. Instead, she led him to their lane. "Gary Lyden, Sharon Keeler, Quentin Helberger, this is Sam Brody, here to take Carla's place."

There were handshakes all around, and for a minute she thought there might be some tension between Sam and Gary, but that was silly. They were adults, and she'd made it clear to both of them, in different ways, that she was in it for the friendship and nothing more.

That she suspected she and Gary were possibly headed down a different path hadn't been discussed. Implied maybe, but not discussed. Which made it even more important for her to be circumspect with Sam, despite the pull.

Sam eyed their shirts. "Did Emma tell you I'm not much of a bowler?"

"That's okay," Sharon said. "None of us are going to be winning any trophies, unless we take best shirt design." She turned around so he could read the back.

"Nicely done." He left it at that, but the look he gave Emma said, *Don't even think about putting me in one of those,* which of course nearly made her giggle.

"Pretty soon, we'll be getting the first round of beers," Sharon said, still sizing up poor Sam. She didn't mean anything by it, but he wouldn't know that. "So you might want to go suit up."

"Yes, ma'am." He glanced at Emma. "So shoes now, then ball, then I'll meet you back here?"

"I'll come with you. I want to pay the rental fee."

He rolled his eyes at her. "Really?" Then he walked away, shaking his head.

"Where's Deanna?" Quentin asked.

"Late, as usual," Gary said, but he was looking at Emma. When she met his gaze, his expression turned quizzical, like it had yesterday in the faculty lounge.

She simply smiled and sat down, certain that once the game started, everything would be fine. Completely fine.

THE ENTIRE PEP TALK Sam had given himself on the way to the bowling alley about how this friendship thing was going to be difficult but doable had already gone down the toilet. He'd only been there five minutes and he was in trouble. Although he'd realized the truth the moment he'd seen Emma in her oversize bowling shirt with her shining hair and her beautiful smile.

All he could think of was what it had felt like to be inside her. The sound of her climax, the taste of her sex. His cock twitched in interest and it was a good thing he couldn't follow his instinct to pull her into his arms.

Friends. Yeah. It was going to take some serious commitment to pull this off. Not just tonight, either. The kind of commitment he'd already pledged to his career transition. Did he even have the fortitude to tackle both? Or should he cut and run from Emma? Maybe losing her entirely would be easier in the end.

The thought made him ill.

"Size?"

Sam paid for his shoes and went back to the torture of being so close and yet so far. He'd felt a lot like this when Danny had been alive, but she'd been completely off-limits, so the discomfort then was more like a paper cut compared to the knife in his gut now. Still, he smiled as he looked for a decent ball, trying to recall if he'd prefer the fifteen pounder over the sixteen.

When he joined his team, another woman had arrived, which brought their party to six. Sharon, who was sitting next to Emma chattering away, looked to be in her late thirties, and reminded him of the woman who played

Leonard's mom on *The Big Bang Theory* and wore bright red socks with comic cow faces on them.

The new arrival came at him with a smile. "I'm Deanna," she said. "Have you met everyone?"

"Everyone but you." He put down his shoes and shifted the ball to his left hand. "Sam Brody. Friend of Emma's here to fill in for—"

"Carla." Deanna shook his hand. "I'm getting the first round. What would you like?"

"Heineken if they've got it." He reached for his wallet, but Deanna stopped him.

"We pay to the kitty. Gary's in charge of that."

Sam's attention moved to him. He was certain this was the man who ran with Emma in the mornings. He was reasonably good-looking if a woman didn't mind the geeky type. The horn-rims were now a thing, so he could just be a hipster, but nope, his jeans weren't tight enough for that. Besides, he was older. Mid-thirties? Cheap haircut, not military. Didn't have the posture for it. Wore an ironic half smile, but it was too soon to tell if that was a trademark or merited by the conversation.

Sam didn't like him.

"What's that frown?" Emma said, coming up on his right side. "We haven't even started yet."

"I hadn't realized I was frowning." He sat down to switch shoes. He found this part of bowling creepy as hell, but he didn't say anything about it. Until he got a load of Emma's feet. "Are those bowling shoes? They look like running shoes."

"Ah, yes, they are. They're mine. They match my ball."

The shoes in question were black and neon pink. The stitching on the back of her shirt had that same pink, and now looking over at the return, he knew which ball was hers. It was just like Emma to go all-out, to make a statement that was as vibrant as her personality. "They suit you."

"I can't say the same for yours, sadly."

His rentals were tan and ugly and looked as if they'd been made in the '50s. "True."

"Hurry, though, because we're about to start. You can have two practice shots. You'll go after Quentin and before me."

"Okay. I'm also supposed to pay for the beer?"

"Don't worry about it." She stood up. "I'm going to help Deanna with the drinks, but I'll be back in a flash."

Sam checked out Quentin, who wore a wedding ring, like Sharon had, although he doubted they were married to each other. Gary didn't have any jewelry but a watch. Quentin was a tall guy, very thin, had a little goatee thing happening.

Deanna was closer in age to Emma. She was a pretty brunette, full figured and knew how to work it. He got a good vibe from her. If things started to get weird between him and Emma, he might feel safe talking to Deanna.

Then there were beers all around, and he was surprised to find Emma had gone for a Miller Lite instead of her usual soft drink. But he clicked his bottle to all the other bottles. The overhead lights dimmed, except to illuminate the lanes themselves. Some guy said a short welcome to the crowd, then the music started. It was classic country, not as loud as that midnight alley he'd been to, but you had to raise your voice. Also not his favorite.

He didn't embarrass himself on the practice runs, which was great, but he wasn't going to increase their average, either. Gary got a strike.

When the real games started, he found himself seated between Emma and Deanna. That was fine by him, although Deanna sat a lot closer to him than Emma did.

Every time she put her hand down on the plastic bench, he wanted to squeeze it. When she went to take her turn, his gaze never wavered. She captivated him with her stride, and, Jesus, when she bent over in those jeans, one leg crossed over the other as her arm made a perfect arc, he really struggled.

His game was okay. He wanted to be better than Gary, but he wasn't. Damned if he'd pout about it, though. He smiled, talked to everyone, ordered a second beer.

So did Emma, which was not like her at all. Maybe this friend business wasn't so simple for her, either. She'd been acting cool, keeping things light, not touching. Making sure they didn't accidentally brush shoulders or hands or anything.

The way Gary looked when she started on her second drink told Sam more than he wanted to know. Gary knew that beer got her tipsy quicker than the hard stuff. His gaze was downright proprietary.

If Emma thought Gary was simply a friend, Gary didn't share the sentiment. He wanted her. God knew, Sam understood, but it still made his blood rise, because Gary was already in Emma's intimate circle. Had been for a while.

As Sam was making his approach to release the ball, it occurred to him that he was the interloper in this drama. It startled him into a gutter ball, but he didn't give a damn about that. What if Gary was the right kind of guy for Emma? For all Sam disliked him, he might be a hell of a nice fellow. A steady man with a steady job, who didn't yearn to be something he couldn't. Who lived a nice nine-to-five life, and had mutual friends and shared a love of teaching.

What if Sam had walked in, and this chemical reaction he and Emma had for each other was a kink in the machine, a fly in the ointment? No, Emma had married a pilot. The total opposite of the type of man Sam imagined Gary to be. Surely she wouldn't settle for another teacher.

He looked at her sipping a drink she shouldn't be having. Her gaze bouncing from him to Gary to him. Sharon was talking to her, but Emma was only paying slight attention if any. She was nervous. Not just because of what they'd done Saturday night.

The last thing Sam wanted was to make Emma's life worse. If nothing else, she didn't deserve any more grief than she'd already gone through.

Maybe he just needed to leave her alone. The idea didn't go down easy.

It was his turn again, and this time he did well. Emma followed, and tension was high, mostly because the team was close to breaking their own record, which was all due to Gary's excellent play. And the fact that Emma was drunk. Not falling down, but she definitely wobbled.

The first ball went straight to the gutter. Sam stood and walked closer, concerned that she might fall. She took her time with the second, and much to everyone's surprise, she got a spare. Every pin down.

Before he knew what was happening, she had jumped into his arms and he was swinging her around as she laughed with absolute glee, delight making her shine while he grinned like an idiot. His steps slowed, and their eyes met. The music dimmed as well as the lights, along with everything that wasn't Emma. He wasn't spinning anymore, except for his head, dizzy with wanting her. Needing her.

She leaned toward him, and he tilted his head.

The next sound was a gasp like a thunderclap, and it was bright and loud and real, and they'd almost…nearly… He let her down. Her blush tried to match her bowling ball, and he had to duck his head until the heat dissipated.

"Good game, everyone!" Sharon was standing between them somehow, leading Emma away. "I don't know about anyone else, but I'm too tired to go to the lounge."

"Me, too," Gary said, not sounding at all happy about their triumph. "I'll wrap things up here, and, Emma, I think I should take you home. You shouldn't be driving."

"That's all right," Sam said, practically speaking over Gary's words. "I'll get her home safely."

Emma looked at him, then turned to look at Gary. Her eyes widened and her mouth opened but no response came out.

"THANK YOU," EMMA SAID as she and Sharon walked out to the parking lot. Sharon had stepped in before Emma's inability to say or do anything had become a heretofore unknown level of awkward.

Things hadn't improved much during the ten minutes it took for the bowling portion of the evening to end. Sam had played it cool, acting as if he'd never offered her a ride, as if everything was hunky-dory. She'd thanked him for filling in for Carla, and he'd been gracious about that, too. Gary had done almost as well, but there had been a rather accusatory gaze just before she'd left. At least she was used to feeling sick with guilt, so she knew what to expect.

Sharon pointed her remote at her four-door sedan behind them. It was so quiet Emma heard the locks click open. Emma hurried to climb into the passenger seat and buckle herself in. While Sharon was busy reversing out of the stall, Emma glanced around the parking lot until she saw Sam approach his Mustang. He'd been late and parked on the street. Gary was nowhere she could see. Emma wondered how she ever could have thought inviting Sam along was a good idea.

Sharon grinned. "Well, that was fun."

Emma moaned. "It was horrible."

"Relax, it wasn't all that bad. You'll be fine."

Emma laid her head back and closed her eyes. No, it wasn't fine at all. "We could drive around the block and come back for my car after everyone is gone. Believe me, I'm not tipsy anymore."

"And miss my chance to find out about Sam? No way. I have you captive, and I'm taking full advantage."

"There's really nothing to tell." Her cheeks and ears burned, but it was dark enough Sharon couldn't see. Yes, she and Sharon were friends, but not the kind that discussed their sex lives.

"How long has he been here?"

"Um, let's see…a week or so? We had dinner the second night he arrived so that's…yeah, about a week now."

Met with a lengthy silence, Emma turned to her friend. They'd stopped for a red light, and Sharon was staring at her. "What?"

"You never said."

"I told you. He's an old friend. That's all," Emma said, resisting the urge to squirm. "He and Danny went to the Academy together."

"Ah. I see." Sharon watched the light change to green and drove.

"Why are you being all cryptic?"

"Oh, nothing. It's just that you've clearly known him for a long time. You and Sam are friends, too."

"Yes, we are." Her defensive tone made her wince, and she quickly turned to look out her window.

"So you two kept in touch?"

"No, but that was my fault. I pushed him away after Danny's death. It was a bad time. I—" She sighed, unable to remember how much she'd told Sharon. Even though their relationship had evolved into something nice and comfortable over the past two years, she'd still been care-ful how much she'd said about Danny.

"I can only imagine," Sharon said, driving slowly, which wasn't unusual, just a pain in the butt when Emma didn't want to talk.

"The truth is I'd been planning on getting a divorce. Danny died before I had a chance to tell him. He hadn't made the move to Alamo yet."

Sharon's soft "Oh, honey" made Emma swallow around a lump in her throat. She wasn't sure why she'd blurted that out. Maybe it was the beer. Or maybe she was just so tired of carrying that secret around she'd had to let it go.

"Does Sam know that?"

Emma shook her head. "He'd probably hate me if he knew. Danny was his closest friend. Along with their buddy John, who's at Nellis now. They were like brothers."

"I know it's none of my business, and it's fine if you don't want to tell me, but why did you want the divorce?"

"Pilots. A certain kind of pilot, they're a different breed. Smart and exciting and living for the charge and the adren-aline… It was intoxicating in the beginning. Like living in an adventure story. But it turned out that Danny didn't quite have enough room for me and the air force and fly-ing. I came in second too many times. But the kicker was that I couldn't imagine him as a father, you know? Kids and Danny didn't fit."

"Didn't you say that, what's his name—Vince—was a flyboy?"

"Yeah, but I didn't know that when I met him."

"You went out with him again, though."

"Nope. I realized he was too much like Danny and ended things before they got started."

"Gary'd make a good dad," Sharon said, and if she was

trying to be subtle, she'd failed. "He may not burn as bright as a fighter jock, but he'd keep you warm for a long time."

"You do realize Gary and I aren't dating."

Sharon didn't say a thing, but then she didn't have to. Of course she knew because she'd invited them separately to barbecues and theme parties at her house. Even when all the other guests were couples. She hadn't been pushy about throwing them together, so Emma had never said anything. Although perhaps she should have. She'd hate that Gary had gotten the wrong message when Emma herself didn't know what she wanted yet.

As they pulled up to her place, Sharon put the car in Park, then turned to her. "Be careful, kiddo. Think it through. You deserve the best. Someone who'll put you first."

Emma thought about that sports bike. A man who wanted a marriage and family wouldn't risk his life on something so foolish. Now, why couldn't she remember that when it counted?

9

THE PARKING at Alameda Park was crazy, but that wasn't much of a surprise considering the Fall Festival was a pretty big event for Alamo. A ton of booths were set up, mostly arts and crafts, but there were live shows on the big stage, food of the state fair variety and lots of play areas for the little ones.

The only part that interested Sam was that Emma was here, working the funnel-cake booth with her fellow English teachers. She hadn't mentioned it at bowling, but Deanna had asked him to come by. He'd told himself it had probably slipped Emma's mind, but now he was wondering if he should've stayed away.

Well, he was already here, with nothing else to do on a Saturday. That didn't mean he had to get in her face. He'd check things out, keep his distance until he figured out if his being here was okay or not.

As he made his way through the park, the loudspeakers blared a bad rendition of "Puff the Magic Dragon" sung by a grammar school choir, and the air was thick with a mix of scents both cloying and appetizing at the same time. Sam hadn't been hungry all morning, but now he was thinking homemade tamales might hit the spot.

After he found Emma. After he figured out what to say to her.

The night at the bowling alley had managed to multiply his confusion by the power of ten. There was no doubt Gary was interested in Emma. Sam had nearly convinced himself that the math teacher would be a good choice for her. A better choice than Sam, at least.

Then there'd been that moment after Emma's spare. The chemistry between them had been undeniable and potent. Jesus, he still wanted her. The memories of her in his bed were going to haunt him forever. Why did their first time have to be on the brand-new mattress? Sometimes life could be very unfair.

The funnel-cake booth came into view and, just his luck, the first person he saw was his old buddy Gary. What the hell was he doing there? He wasn't even in the English department. Didn't the man have anything better to do with his time?

There was Sharon, as well, but she was taking off her apron. Emma wasn't visible yet, and as he walked closer he realized the group of people he'd seen by the booth weren't just mingling, they were in line. A long one.

The crowd made it difficult to get close enough to see the whole booth. It was jammed inside the box on wheels, and it didn't look very pleasant. Two big trays were boiling oil, and it had to be hot as Hades, especially considering the booth was enclosed in glass.

Emma stepped up to the window, sliding a huge paper plate holding a cake with a lot of goop and whipped cream on it. Also a soda. Her smile made something inside him ache.

Watching her like this reminded him of her waitress days. She never stopped, hardly ever took a break. If something wasn't ready fast enough, she'd go back behind the bar and help out, sometimes mixing drinks, sometimes cooking. The owners of the Rusty Nail loved her. Everyone did. But when she met Danny, lightning had struck.

He remembered that day, but his most vivid memory of that time and place was the night Emma announced that she and Danny had decided to get married.

Two things had hit Sam within seconds. First, that they had to be nuts to get married so young and without knowing where the air force would send them. And that he was deeply jealous.

Unfortunately, both of those conclusions had come back to him with a vengeance. She had been too young to marry Danny. And no one was like her. Every other woman he'd gone out with had fallen short. That was why he couldn't just let it go. If there was any chance at all that they could be together...

He'd gotten as close as he wanted to for now. He watched her hustle, pouring batter, taking orders, grinning with enthusiasm and humor. She turned at something Gary said, and Sam's heart thudded in his chest as the bastard reached over and pushed some stray hairs from her cheek. Emma's laughter rose above the sound of the crowd until the next musical number started. She bumped Gary's shoulder with her own, and he gave her a look that made her laugh again.

What the hell was Sam doing? He should have bought a clue the other night when Emma hadn't been able to choose between them. Emma had said she and Gary weren't an item, but that was just a matter of time. Once again, someone else had gotten to her first.

The thought brought a stab of guilt with it. Naturally he'd never told Danny that he'd had a thing for his girlfriend, his wife. Never told John, either. It had been a shameful secret, and he'd done all he could not to think about her. To fill the emptiness with different women, flying, doing whatever he could to get his blood moving.

But she'd never left his thoughts completely. When he'd found out he was being transferred to Alamogordo, he'd tried hard not to take it as a sign. What an idiot. It was time to leave. Make a quick exit. She'd never know he was there.

Before he'd even taken five steps, a bundle of energy ran headlong into his side. Sam stumbled, but caught himself before he fell. In a neat trick he probably couldn't have duplicated if he tried, he also managed to stop a soccer ball and the little boy from taking a header.

"Hey, that's mine."

The kid must have been around seven or so. Skinny as a rail with a close-cropped head of black curls and big brown eyes, he lunged for the ball and almost tripped again. His feet were the problem. They'd sprouted before the rest of him could catch up.

"Take it easy there, big guy." Sam put his toe underneath the ball and flipped it into his left hand. "Here you go." Sam looked around to see if someone was watching the kid, but no one seemed interested. "Are you supposed to be here by yourself?"

"I'm playing soccer with the sixth graders. They let me play because my brother said so. I get to kick the ball if I chase it when it goes out of bounds."

"And where is your brother?"

The boy looked behind him, then stopped. Turned to his left, then his right, then back to center, and Sam could see he was getting a little panicked.

Crouching down, he put his hand on the boy's shoulder. "Don't worry…we'll find them. Let's see if we can get out of this crowd first, okay? Someone will know where the sixth-grade soccer players are."

"Okay. They need the ball back. He'll be mad if I'm late."

"You don't worry about that. What's your name?"

"Elijah."

"Nice to meet you. I'm Sam." He let Elijah carry the ball while lightly keeping his hand on the boy's shoulder as they headed back in the direction he'd come from. Soon enough, they found the soccer field, but the sixth graders weren't waiting for their lost ball. They were in the middle of a game that looked far too rough for someone Elijah's size.

"Do you see your brother?"

Elijah wiped his nose with the back of his arm. "He's over there," he said, not even bothering to point.

"What about your parents?"

He nodded toward a picnic area, where a tall woman was holding a baby and looking frantic.

"Come on, she's worried. Let's run."

Elijah's mother was grateful but scared, and Sam didn't stick around for the aftermath. He figured the kid was more upset about not being able to play than getting in trouble.

He walked in the direction of his car, slowly this time, trying not to let his mood send him into a tailspin. The whole point of caring about someone was to want the best for them. He'd always hoped Emma would be happy. Only, he wanted to be the one to make her that way.

Almost to his car, he heard his name. He turned to find Emma jogging toward him without the big apron she'd worn in the truck. He couldn't hold back a smile at her pink-striped T-shirt and plaid shorts. So very Emma.

"Where are you going?" she asked, breathless from her run in the September heat.

Sam shook his head, trying not to stare at the tiny damp hairs plastered to her temple. He wanted to sweep them back, erase Gary's touch. "Home."

She ended up wiping her forehead with the side of her hand. "God, it's unbearable. The cart is air-conditioned."

"You shouldn't get overheated. Maybe you should go back."

Her hand stilled in midair. "What's going on? Why didn't you come up and say hello? I saw you, but then you left with that little boy."

He should send her away, send her back to Gary, but when it came to Emma, Sam had no willpower. "Come to the car. I've got cold water."

She nodded, walked beside him. "Was it too awkward the other night? I swear it was the beer. I don't know why it gets to me so quickly. I could probably drink you under the table with tequila, but two beers and I'm an idiot."

"Thursday night was fine…bowling was fun," he said. "It was nice to meet your friends." He clicked open his car doors and the trunk. The small ice chest was stocked with water bottles and soda. He grabbed a couple of the waters and opened hers.

"Thanks," she said, and took a long drink. "Then why were you leaving without a word?"

The confession sat heavy in his chest. Instead of coming out with it, he got behind the wheel and turned over the engine, pushing the air vents toward the passenger seat, then opening her window halfway. "Get in before you melt."

She did. The moment she closed her door, he realized it wasn't the smartest move. Up close, he could see how hurt she looked. How confused.

"You were busy. The line was long—"

Her stare didn't soften so much as give up. "So what was all that with the kid?"

Grabbing on to the life raft she'd tossed him, he smiled. "His big brother was trying to get rid of him. Kicked the ball into the crowd. The little guy got confused. We went to find his folks."

"They must have been grateful."

"Mad, more like it. These days it's got to be scary going to a public event with more than one child to keep track of. They can disappear so fast."

"That was really nice, Sam." Her expression was odd, not one he recalled seeing before, but her soft smile...he loved that smile.

"What was nice?"

"Staying with him until he spotted his parents and knowing they'd be worried. You could've just handed him the ball."

"That surprises you?"

"I've never really seen you with kids. And I know you're an only child, so...well, who knew you could be so empathetic?"

"Gee, thanks."

"No." Laughing, she briefly touched his arm, and it was pretty sad how the casual contact got to him. "I didn't mean it like that...honest."

"Hey, I like kids. I sort of figured I'd have at least one by now."

If she'd looked confused before, now she seemed completely bewildered. She drew back and gave him a long look.

"What? It's not that weird. Lots of men want children."

"No, you're right. Lots do. But I never pictured..." She took another quick sip of water. "So why were you running off, Sam?"

"I don't much like being a third wheel," he admitted. "You and Gary look comfortable together. He seems like a nice guy."

Her eyebrows shot up. "Gary and I are friends. Nothing more."

"I don't think he got the memo on that."

She drank some more water, and he knew a stall tactic when he saw it. "I've known him for over a year. He is a nice guy. I like him.... I like hanging out with him. A few times I thought we might be headed somewhere," she said carefully. "But there's no spark, no chemistry. Or it would have surfaced by now."

He should have argued with her, but those little hairs at her temple were teasing him. Before he could stop himself, he brushed them back, his thumb lingering on the warmth of her skin.

Just as he was going to pull away, her hand gripped his wrist. She leaned closer, and he mirrored her, knowing exactly what was about to happen. "Don't," he said. "Friends don't kiss the way I want to kiss you right now."

She nodded, moving his hand along with her head. "I know. We should stop." But she didn't.

He didn't.

With one hand trapped, and one on the edge of her seat, he closed the connection, completing the circuit. The spark could have lit up the city.

She tasted like sugar and cinnamon. Sam struggled not to push too hard, to let her set the pace, but when her grip tightened and her tongue thrust between his lips, all bets were off. He kissed her back, hard and deep, and felt her shudder. A moan started low in his throat, and he didn't even try to squash it. Didn't care that they were making out in the parking lot like a couple of high school kids. Lacking chemistry clearly wasn't their problem.

She pulled back, breathing hard. Her gaze was wide and dark as she stared into his eyes. He was sure she'd leave.

That it was over before it had begun, but then he leaned forward and she didn't turn away.

Finally, she let go of his wrist, and he was able to run his hand over her back. When she gripped him again at his nape, he smiled, never stopping the push-pull of their mouths. She wanted him there, steady and sure, and she wanted to keep the fire burning.

The hell with Gary, the hell with being friends. This was what he wanted. Needed. Emma to be his.

When she finally pulled away for real, it felt like a blow. She looked ravished. He hadn't realized his hand had been in her hair. Her lips were puffy and slick, more like she'd run a mile than cooled off in a car.

"I have to go back to the booth."

He nodded even as he thought about tearing out of the parking lot and stealing her away. That is, if he hadn't completely drained the battery by running it in this heat.

"Come over tonight."

"I can't. I'm working late here."

"Tomorrow, then."

The look on her face told him that was also a no. "I've made plans."

"All day?"

She looked away, and he knew.

"Your plans are with Gary."

She put off her reply by fetching her water bottle from the floor. "We're going for a run."

"After that?" he asked, knowing he wasn't going to be happy with her answer.

"Not here. It's a trail a couple of hours away. Then lunch."

"So it's not a run. It's a date."

She opened her mouth, but once again, just like the last time she'd had to make a choice, she offered no argument.

"Okay, then," he said, the fight slipping away. For him, it seemed Emma would always be just out of reach. "I can see where he could be the right guy for you. A spark doesn't make a relationship. There's more to it than that."

"Sam—"

"They're probably worried about you now. You should get back to the booth."

With a sigh and nod, she got out of the Mustang. He didn't watch her walk away.

IT WAS ONLY THREE in the afternoon, and Emma was already back in Alamo after her outing with Gary. She'd rushed it. She hadn't planned to; in fact, she'd meant to use the day with him to readjust her expectations, to get herself back on track. It had seemed so appropriate, given they'd gone to the Cloud Climbing Rail Trail out in Cloudcroft. The run itself was easy, but the scenery was outstanding, part of a large system of old railroad tracks that crossed an old gorge and trestle bridge.

Gary had gone to a lot of trouble, bringing a full picnic lunch. They'd found an idyllic spot with great shade and a cool breeze. He'd brought a decent bottle of wine, crusty French bread with artisan cheeses and smoked meats, chilled artichokes and fresh veggies.

When she saw the spread, the picnic blanket, the way Gary was looking at her, she knew. Sam was right. It had been a date. Or at least a date calling card.

Although she wanted to tell Gary that no, she didn't feel that way about him, she hadn't said a word. If she wanted to be completely honest, she'd admit that up until two weeks ago she'd entertained the possibility. Sam had nailed it when he remarked that a spark didn't make a relationship. How many times had she told herself that? That was why she'd been taking things slowly with Gary. Her plan had been to fall gently. To not get swept away in a tidal wave of passion and wild sex, but to walk into a relationship with both eyes open and both feet firmly on the ground. Great in theory.

Today she'd tried. She really had. She'd smiled and listened to his stories, asked him questions, laughed at his jokes, and with each bite of the terrific lunch he'd thoughtfully provided, each childhood tale, her perfectly reasonable plan had been derailed.

If she didn't do something drastic, she was going to get herself into one hell of a mess.

Everything Sharon had told her that night in the car was true. Gary would be a fantastic father. He'd stick with her through thick and thin. He had every quality she'd written on her wish list. The one that wasn't filled with rock stars and fighter jocks, that is.

Her list had matured. She wanted stability. Common sense. Someone who would never consider getting any kind of motorcycle, let alone one that could go over one hundred eighty miles an hour. He'd put her first. The family first.

The man she needed was safe and sane. He was good-looking, but in a modest way. He was fit because it was the smart thing to do for a long, healthy life.

He was Gary.

The question was, how was she supposed to switch off the way she wanted Sam? Not just wanted him but craved him. Which made her the biggest hypocritical fool of all. He was her fast bike, the flame she knew she shouldn't touch. Did she truly have to get burned twice to learn?

And what was she going to do about Gary? He was too nice a man, too good a friend, to keep dangling. She would never want to hurt him, but it might already be too late.

No more. Even if all she could tell him was that she

wasn't ready, she had to let him know. She'd want the same thing in return.

Of course, there was one solution to the Sam situation, if she was brave enough to follow through with it. Tell him the friendship wasn't working. That seeing him wasn't a good idea.

He'd know it was a lie. But Sam was a gentleman down to the core, and he'd never call her on it if she told him with true conviction.

Could she, though? Was that what she wanted?

God, it was too much, and she needed to just go home, pour herself a cold lemonade and zone out in front of the TV. She'd watch a movie. Not a romance. That was for sure. *The Da Vinci Code*. That would work. Or that documentary the Frozen something. After a nice long shower, and once she was in her pajamas, she'd feel one hundred percent better. Refreshed. Logical. She'd be able to see the long game, not get all caught up in the kissing and the heavy breathing and what it felt like when Sam's arms were around her and she could feel the pounding of his heart because it matched her own.

Shit.

She stopped at the red light and flipped on her right-turn signal. The second the light changed to green, she made a left instead. And without a single shred of rational thought, headed straight for Sam's apartment complex.

God, she was hopeless.

Turning right would've taken her to the safety of her cozy little ranch home. She couldn't even trust herself for one minute.

Pulling into a parking spot, she turned off the engine and let her head rest on the steering wheel. She was in trouble. Big, big trouble. Now she was even finding her way to him like a homing pigeon. She'd probably be able to use echolocation next.

Maybe she was here for a reason. Maybe it was to tell him, once and for all, that they couldn't be together. That he was all wrong for her in every respect. Except, that wasn't true, was it? There was so much to admire about Sam. His sense of honor and duty. His kindness and his loyalty.

Well, the bike. The motorcycle was a problem, one she couldn't ignore.

And the underlying personality that made him want the bike and the jets and the skydiving in the first place.

She needed someone who was safe. Who would be a good dad for their children. She needed someone to be *there.* A man who wanted to be with her more than his buddies. And wasn't always looking for the next big rush.

She got out of the car, tucked her keys in her pocket and headed to his door. A light was on inside, and she heard the TV when she pressed her ear up against the wood.

At her knock, things got quiet, and a moment later she heard the knob turn. The look on his face was careful, but there was surprise in his eyes.

"This isn't working," she said.

He stared at her. Then he stepped back to give her room to pass. "Would you like to come in?"

She nodded, stepped over the threshold and waited for him to close the door. When he faced her again, she repeated, "This isn't working."

"What, exactly, isn't working?"

"This friendship."

"Oh." The surprise left. In fact, the very life of him seemed to vanish from his gaze. "I see."

"It's not working because I can't stop thinking about kissing you," she said, closing her eyes and just giving in.

"I keep thinking about last Saturday night, and remembering every detail. Waking up next to you, holding you. I want that. More than I should. But it's true, and I can't seem to stop wanting it."

Looking up at him now, there was a whole different man in front of her. Coming closer. Pulling her into his arms and kissing the doubt straight out of her.

"Don't scare me like that," he said, when he finally grabbed a breath. "Never again."

She met his gaze, and knew there was one more thing she had to do. The hardest thing. If it blew up in her face, well, better to know now than later. She held up her hand, put it on his chest.

He let his grip loosen, and then let her go, although not far. "Tell me. Please. Whatever it is, I can't—"

"I was going to divorce Danny. I planned on telling him when he got to Alamo. But he died. And I never told anyone. I was going to leave him, Sam. I'd already started the paperwork."

The way he looked at her… She stopped breathing.

10

WHATEVER SAM HAD THOUGHT Emma was going to say, it wasn't that. He'd thought their marriage could withstand anything. Sometimes he'd wondered how Emma could deal with Danny's absences and wild streak. Or if she suspected he might not have been faithful. Or even why Danny would choose to hang out with pilots instead of his wife, but he figured they'd worked out their own lives and it wasn't his business. "You've never told anyone?"

Emma shook her head slowly, her large eyes dark and wide. But it was the way she was playing with her hands that let him know just how nervous she was about her confession. Since they'd reconnected, Sam hadn't noticed her fidgeting with her fingers like she used to back in the day.

"I've felt so guilty over it," she said, her voice catching.

"Oh, Emma. I'm sorry things had been rough for you. Even sorrier that you had to carry that burden on your own."

Her lips parted in a sigh, but her body didn't relax.

Wrapping his arms around her, pressing her close with her cheek on his chest, he rocked her gently.

"He was a good man," she mumbled, her breath leaching through the fabric of his T-shirt. "He loved me. He did.

I never doubted that." She gripped the back of his shirt. "He didn't understand that I got lonely sometimes. That I was hoping for a family. Mostly, though, I was tired of being so low in his priorities."

Sam held her even tighter. "I loved Danny like a brother, still do. But he had an ego on him. He craved the spotlight like he craved adrenaline. Hard to compete with that."

Her nod was tiny, but her hands loosened, so he knew something was getting through.

"The important thing now is for you to stop feeling guilty about wanting the kind of life you deserve. You're amazing, Emma, and you'll be a great mother. I can see you with a couple of kids. Danny did love you, you're right. But I think he loved being a fighter pilot even more."

She leaned back, looked up into his eyes. "Really? You knew that?"

Sam nodded, not wanting to tell her that he understood too well that Danny lived for flying. All three of them had. If Sam had married young he probably would have acted the same way, even though he'd like to think otherwise. "He did the best he could. I think he would have been sad to hear you'd wanted a divorce, but he would have understood it, too."

"I'd like to believe that."

He kissed her nose. "Believe it. Whatever else, he'd want you happy. That I can swear to."

She smiled at him, and he bent to kiss her. He licked away the hint of tears on her lips, but he didn't press. More than anything he ached to take her to bed, to comfort her and please her. But she'd just unloaded a heavy pack, and if she needed some time to recuperate then—

"Take me to bed, Sam," she said, her lips a scant inch from his own.

Wasting no time, he led her into the bedroom, where

he started to undress her, but she shook her head. "If you don't mind, I just want to be in bed with you as quickly as possible."

"For the record, no. I don't mind. Take that as a given."

That made her laugh, which was good. Great. He wished he could make all her worries disappear, but at least this one, this guilt she'd had that somehow she'd been selfish or wrong about her marriage, he could mitigate. He'd told her the truth. Danny would want her happy.

All of her clothes were already on his office chair when he stripped out of his jeans and boxers. He had to press on his hardening cock, just for a moment, to relieve the immediate ache, because there was no way not to react to her naked body. It was as if she'd been made to his specifications. Or maybe that was backward. Maybe he'd been so infatuated with Emma for so long that she'd become his ideal. He didn't care which, as long as he could have her.

Not that he was counting his chickens. He hoped they were starting something that would last, but— Screw it. He wasn't going to think about what could go wrong, not when he was crawling between the sheets with his dream woman.

He didn't want to rush this. There was no hurry, despite his rapid heartbeat and the need to be as close to her as possible. "You're right, you know."

"About what?" she asked as she curled around him, straddling his waist. She peppered him with kisses. Nose, cheek, chin, forehead. Random little pecks that ended too quickly. It was like being licked by hummingbirds.

"The friendship thing wasn't working for me, either," he said, letting her have her way. Grinning when she nipped his earlobe. "Not that I wouldn't have kept on trying, but it was sorely testing me."

"I know," she said, just before she licked a swipe across

his lower lip. "I couldn't stop thinking about you. Even during class. One of my students caught me in full blush. Had the nerve to ask me what was making me so pink."

"What did you do?"

"Gave them a pop quiz, that's what. I don't put up with that kind of impudence in my classroom."

He barked a laugh. "That'll show 'em."

"Damn straight." She reared her head back so she could look at him. "But it taught me a lesson. I have to be careful when it comes to you. Once I let you into my thoughts, it's difficult to change gears."

"You don't have to worry about that now. I don't want you to change anything. In fact, I can only encourage you to remember what made you blush so I can be sure to do it again."

"Let's see if you can work that out on your own."

He raised his eyebrows. "A challenge, huh?"

Her grin was pure wicked fun. Not even a hint of sadness remained. "Lucky for you, I've got a late class tomorrow. Feel free to take your time. And be sure to show your work."

"Why, Ms. Lockwood. Will you keep me after class if I get anything wrong?"

Lowering her lips to his, she whispered, "I have great faith in your tenacity and skill." Then she kissed him.

The last thing he cared about was dazzling her with his moves. But he did want to make her happy and satisfied. The kiss deepened, and after all that teasing, the lingering push-pull of their tongues felt like an unbearable luxury. Her low moan sounded a lot like a purr, which was a sign he was on the right track.

He hoped she liked a slow buildup, because that was what he planned on giving her. If he could hold out. His aim was to drive all coherent thoughts from her head, to leave her wrecked by pure pleasure.

First, though, he urged her onto her side so they faced each other. As he continued their interrupted kiss, he brushed his knuckles across the tender flesh of the back of her knees, then turned his hand over and skimmed his palm slowly up her thigh. When he found the curve of her buttock, he lingered, used his knuckles again, just hard enough that it wouldn't tickle.

She squirmed against him, making soft noises. Her open palms were exploring him, too, only she was concentrating on his chest. When she tugged his nipple between her thumb and finger she wasn't the only one squirming.

He moved his touch to the edge of her inner thigh then stopped. Emma arched into his hand. "No fair."

He could have played her for hours, but she let him know she wanted to move more quickly by sliding her hand down and gripping his cock. To further make her point she simply held him. No stroking at all.

Despite the persuasiveness of the gesture he wasn't going to just flip her on her back and attack, although the idea had merit. No, she'd said to show his work, to take his time.

He turned his lowered hand over and ran one finger down to the back of her knee, then around to the front. Still using only a single digit, he traced a path up her vulnerable inner thigh, smiling when the higher he went the wider she spread her legs.

He mapped his way up the side of her folds, maneuvering his position until he had her beautiful breasts in licking distance. A good pilot knew how to press several buttons at once, and he was a damn good pilot. Sucking her left nipple into his mouth, he swirled his tongue while down below he got closer and closer to the wet heat between her legs.

Her wriggles were becoming an issue, but he wasn't the kind of man who buckled under pressure. But when she squeezed his cock, then stroked him with the perfect amount of pressure, he folded like a cheap paper bag.

The one finger became two as he hit moist, hot flesh. From there it was a matter of seconds to find her very hard little clit.

He took her almost soundless gasp as a good sign.

When he pulled back to switch his attention to her neglected breast, he looked up. Her pupils couldn't have been any larger, her lush mouth damp and perfect. She narrowed her gaze, but instead of speaking she loosened her grip and scooted down until she could cup his balls. "Are you trying to drive me insane?"

He frowned. "Trying? We're more than halfway there, wouldn't you say?"

She squeezed. Not hard, simply as a reminder. "Maybe it's time I took the wheel."

His fingers, having never stopped rubbing in gentle circles, pushed inside her, stroking in and out and in harder. "Better?"

She rolled his sack in her palm, then moved back to gripping his shaft. "Remember," she said in a very sketchy voice, "this will count for at least half your final grade."

He sighed. "All right then. I guess I'll have to bring out the big guns."

"So full of yourself."

"No, but you will be." He'd been thinking about the move since he'd begun the slow burn, and now, all the pieces fell together in a move that would have made his hand-to-hand instructors weep. When she looked up at him this time, her head was on the pillow, her arms flung wide, and he was sliding into position between her spread knees.

"Well, okay then," she said. Her panting had accelerated and a flush bloomed on her chest.

"One last bit," he said, before he kissed her silly.

While he struggled to maintain contact he grabbed a condom from the bedside table and had that sucker open in two hot seconds. Once that was accomplished, he bent over her, balancing himself on his straightened arms. "Okay?"

She brought her heels up to dig into the mattress. "God, yes."

His moan must have carried all the way to the base as he entered her up to the root.

EMMA DIDN'T WANT to close her eyes. The sun was going down and golden light bled into the room through the top of his windows, illuminating the bed so she could see his five o'clock shadow, the white of his teeth against his tan skin. But she could barely look away from his eyes. Even now when they were pressed tightly shut, with his chin jutting out, and his panting breaths setting a rhythm that matched his thrusts.

He'd surprised her again. He'd been caring and sweet and funny and hot. Driven her insane with each graze of his finger, turning up the heat until he had her suspended at the cusp of an orgasm.

She couldn't believe she hadn't come yet. She knew she could with him inside her, she had before, and he was hitting exactly the right spot, but not every time. So she remained in limbo. The part that was always over too soon, when her climax was inevitable, when nothing short of a cataclysm could stop the oncoming rush. And Sam held her there, her muscles tense, her heart beating impossibly fast.

She pulsed up as he thrust in, crying out when he rubbed against her oh-so-sensitized clit.

"That's it," he said, speeding up. "Come on, gorgeous.

Don't hold back. Look at you, so hot, so amazing. God, I want to do everything all at once."

Her nails had to be scraping the hell out of his back, but she couldn't seem to stop. It wasn't possible for the pressure to build any more, and yet—

Sam bent down and took her in a fevered kiss, his body trembling as he thrust into her so hard the whole bed moved.

She came apart. Crying out, jerking so hard she tore away from his lips, feeling the release in every cell. He was pressing against her, the tendons of his neck straining, his heat burning her up.

Time slid and dipped. He moved to her side, she struggled for breath, he touched her hand. She must have drifted off, but not for long because the light had gone from gold to orange.

She could feel him everywhere, imprinted forever.

THE NEXT TIME she opened her eyes, it was dark. Her head and his were sharing a pillow. They were touching from shoulders to knees, and at some point Sam had pulled the blankets over them.

She closed her eyes, although she didn't want to fall asleep again, not yet. She considered all the nights she'd gone to bed alone. The mornings her only company had been the alarm. This was different in more ways than the obvious. The second she'd come to consciousness, she'd felt his presence. The scent of sex was there, but so was his scent alone. The bed still smelled more of him than them.

His body was big. Safe in a very primal way. She wasn't a delicate flower, but she could let herself be protected by this man and feel no less strong.

None of that mattered as much as the fact that it was

Sam. She didn't need a man. She wanted Sam. Big difference.

There were issues to deal with, and she wasn't about to run from them, but for the moment all she cared about was sleeping pressed up against Sam Brody.

"You're awake," he said, his voice crackling with sleep.

"How did you know?"

"Spidey sense."

She elbowed him lightly. "Come on. How?"

"Your breathing changed. You grew tense for a bit. And you've moved closer to me."

She hadn't noticed that last part. "So I have. I'm sorry I woke you, though."

He reached over and ran his palm from her neck down her chest, lingering over her breast, and then her hip bone. "You have my permission to wake me anytime."

"You say that now—"

"I didn't promise not to be grumpy about it. Besides, I'm easy. You already know how to render me helpless."

"That's true. I'll keep it in mind."

"Do you need anything," he asked, inching closer still. "Water? A bathroom break?"

"Nope. I'm good."

"Yes, you are," he said, kissing her shoulder. "You were right about the bed."

She smiled. "Beds are very important. Ask anyone who had to share one with her sister. That went on for three years until I was seven."

"I hope it was a big bed."

"Sadly, no," she said. "It's a miracle we both made it out alive."

He hummed for a few seconds, rubbed his thumb over her skin. "I wanted a little brother so bad. I begged my mom. My dad had split when I was three, and she was so busy trying to raise me by herself, she didn't date a whole lot."

She opened her eyes again, but not for long. As much as she wanted to talk to Sam, especially about his life before she'd known him, it had to be very late. "Why did I think your father had died?"

"He might as well have been dead. He wanted nothing to do with us."

"Oh, Sam, I'm sorry. But your mom did a good job by herself."

"It wasn't easy. He never paid child support. He took the trouble to divorce my mother, but only so he could get married again. Start a new family."

"You're kidding."

"Doesn't matter. We did just fine on our own."

"I'll say."

The hum came back, and she knew sleep was going to win any second, but she couldn't help one last question. "The other night you mentioned that you thought you'd get married someday. How come it hasn't happened yet, Sam?"

He got quiet, and just when she thought he'd dozed off, he said, "There was someone back when I was at Hill. You and Danny were at Hill."

"Yeah, he told me about her. What happened?"

His hand moved back up her body, and this time he let it rest on her breast. It felt nice. "She was an air force brat. Colonel's daughter. We were good together, and I thought about making it something permanent."

"But?"

She felt him shrug. "In the end, I couldn't do it. That famous spark we've talked about…it wasn't there, you know? I liked her a lot. But there was no magic."

Just yesterday they'd sat in his Mustang talking about Gary, and Sam had said a spark didn't make a relationship. But clearly it made a difference. "You think there has to be magic?"

He kissed her cheek. "Yeah, I guess I do."

She sighed, and thought about that until she drifted off.

_11_

SAM CHECKED the bathroom again. He'd bought her a case for the toothbrush she'd used last time. He'd stuck it away in a closet half an hour after she'd left. Maybe it would stay this time.

Emma was still sleeping, although he'd have to wake her soon. He'd laid out towels for a shower, a brand-new washcloth, toothpaste. Everything was squared away in there, so he went back to the kitchen. There were pancakes warming in the oven, coffee brewed, OJ if she wanted some.

He sipped from his own mug, then set it down. This acting-crazy business had to stop. Right now. He was an airman. He had dignity and purpose. He was not going to be undone by an after-sex breakfast.

After adjusting the table settings one more time then growling at his idiocy, he headed for the bedroom. Emma might not have to be at school until ten, but he needed to be at the base. It was back to work for him, although classes wouldn't start until Wednesday. Tomorrow was orientation. Today would be setting up his shared office, which amounted to a big crate in the middle of the desert.

They were air-conditioned crates, but from the outside they looked like something from a shipping yard. All sand-colored to blend in to the arid land on which they were parked.

Inside most of them, and there were a hell of a lot, they'd find computer monitors, a couple of big old chairs, joysticks and enough electronics to send a nerd to heaven. The student pilots would sit on the left, and the sensor operators, who monitored the aircraft and weapons system, on the right. They would interact with the most vividly realistic images of terrain available on the planet as they learned how to navigate, observe, collect data and deploy armaments.

When they graduated, they would move to different bays, only the exercises would no longer be simulated.

But all that could wait, because the woman in his bed was moving, and he got a bird's-eye view of what she looked like waking up.

He wanted to rip off his uniform and climb in next to her.

"You're already dressed," she said, her arms flung high in a luxurious stretch that spread all the way down to her toes. He knew that for a fact, as he'd watched her stiffen beneath the covers.

"You know the military. They just hate it when you show up for work naked."

"I'd like to see that, actually. If you wouldn't mind."

He grinned. "For you? Anything. But you might want to know that there are actual pancakes ready in the oven, and coffee and orange juice in the fridge. Eggs, too, if you want."

"God, how did you know I'd be starving to death?"

"I didn't feed you last night."

"Right," she said. "Totally worth it."

"If you want to shower, go ahead. I don't have fresh clothes, but everything else is at your disposal."

Her smile lit him up inside. "Damn shame about that whole work thing."

He groaned, almost moved toward the bed, but stopped himself. "You…are trouble," he said, his stern look undermined by the rasp in his voice.

She smiled wider and he turned away. He had to. She was far too tempting, and he couldn't trust himself any longer. He busied himself in the living room, turning on the stupid-ass fountain. Then reading the titles of the books on his shelf.

When he figured it was safe, he went to the kitchen and waited. It should have been no big deal. He was a ten-year veteran of the hurry-up-and-wait air force. But he paced like an expectant…boyfriend.

At least he hoped he was no longer in the friend zone. Because, damn, last night had been about as good as it ever got. The only thing better would be more of the same.

When she finally arrived in her shorts and T-shirt, she didn't even look at the table. She just threw her arms around his neck and kissed him until he got dizzy. He hadn't even realized he'd picked her up until she kicked him in the ankle.

"Sorry," she murmured, looking anything but.

"It's okay. Now sit that gorgeous bottom down and let me serve you breakfast. Coffee first?"

"Need you ask?"

He poured her a mug, not the one with the boobs, then brought out the pancakes.

"What's on the agenda today?" she asked, reaching for the milk he'd set on the table. "First class?"

"Prep for the first class. Getting my desk squared away, along with the study plans."

"Sounds familiar."

"I'll undoubtedly come begging for help when classes

begin. Although I did some of that during my training. It's different, though, when it's the real deal."

"Just try and do name mnemonics at first. It'll automatically make the students like you better if you remember their names, and they'll want to please you more."

"These guys are pilots. I don't think that trick will apply."

She gave him a funny look, which he couldn't quite read, but it still made him wish he'd kept his mouth shut. But airmen, pilots in particular, were accustomed to being addressed by their rank and surname.

"Oh, right. Yeah. I forgot we were talking about pilots and not mere mortals."

"Hey."

Emma shook her head. "I'm kidding."

"You're not. But I understand. Officers can be…a unique challenge. But I like your thinking. Any other tips?"

"Yep. How about we make plans for you to buy me that dinner you promised?"

The kick he got from knowing there would be more of Emma took the sting out of her comment. It had to be difficult for an outsider to put up with all the military crap, especially where pilots were concerned. Modesty wasn't exactly a sought-after trait. "How does tonight work for you?"

Emma ate some more of her pancake, then shook her head. "I've got an online workshop tonight."

"That's okay. Fine." He put down his fork. "Can I see you after?"

She smiled again, and he felt her toes running up his calf. "I think we can work something out."

"It's going to be a long damn day." He reached for her foot and almost caught it before she pulled back, trying not to laugh with her mouth full. "I need to ask you something."

"Yes?"

"Does this mean we're going steady?"

The look she gave him was almost perfect. But he couldn't help catch the tiny hesitation, the darting glance. "I think we've both ruled out the friends-only thing."

"But…?"

"I haven't heard that stupid term in a million years, although I can't think of one that's better. So, yes. We're going steady. However, I have to clear up some things on my end before we take out an ad in the paper."

"Is that something people do in Alamogordo?"

She flicked a crumb at him. "You've been my boyfriend for less than five minutes, and you're already giving me sass?"

"I'll show you sass," he said, standing up and giving her no time to prepare before he swept her into a kiss that almost sent them both tumbling.

He had her, though. And he wasn't about to let her fall. He might not be having the career he'd always wanted, but if he played his cards right, he just might end up winning after all.

THE RERUNS OF THE NIGHT and this morning had been a continuous, wonderful loop all the way back to her place. But once she stepped inside, the rainbows and unicorns stopped. She had to speak to Gary. Today, if at all possible.

He already knew something was up. She'd hurried through their day at Cloudcroft, had shown her hand at bowling. Gary hadn't even questioned her disappearance from the funnel-cake booth at the festival. In fact, he'd asked her why Sam hadn't come to sample a treat for himself. Coming from another guy it might've been a snide remark implying he'd seen them in the car. But not from Gary. That was what made what she had to tell him so difficult. He was at heart a decent man and a good friend.

As soon as she'd finished changing clothes and pulling all her things together for her afternoon class, she called him. He would be in his office at the moment, and she was pretty sure she'd get his voice mail. Nope.

"I thought you might have come in early today," he said. "Late night?"

"Not particularly," she said, wincing. He might have meant that innocently but then again maybe he was capable of being snide. "Can you meet me for coffee after our two o'clock class?"

He didn't say anything for a drawn-out moment. "Sure. X-Presso?"

"Yes, great. See you then." She disconnected, but didn't move from the center of the kitchen as she tried to figure out what she was going to say to him that wouldn't hurt their friendship.

GARY ARRIVED FIRST, and he'd already bought her a cup of chai and found them a table. If she'd gotten there before him, she'd have ordered his mocha with a shot. There were surprisingly few airmen in the base-exchange café. She was glad. This was a conversation best not overheard.

"So, I'm guessing this is about Sam?"

She didn't bother to outright deny it, although his declaration messed up the opening she'd rehearsed. "Actually, it's more about me than Sam. I didn't expect him to come back into my life. Now that he is, things have gotten complicated."

"Complicated how?"

She sipped her drink to cover her surprise. This wasn't going the way she'd imagined. "I don't want things to

change between you and me. You're one of my best friends.
We've gotten to know each other well over the last year,
and I like you. A lot."

"But…?"

"Sam is important to me, as well. I'm not sure how it's
going to wind up. Maybe friendship, maybe more."

"I see," he said, nodding. He seemed disappointed, but
not as much as she'd expected. In fact, his whole attitude
was disconcerting.

She leaned back in the uncomfortable plastic chair.
"You understand that I don't want to change the status
quo. With us, I mean."

"Yeah, I do. I get why things seem complicated. Sam's
an old friend. The two of you share a lot of history. And
hell, he's a good-looking man. A fighter pilot. I imagine
it's very exciting to be with him."

"I'm sorry, what?" Emma didn't see where he was going
with this. Gary wasn't a vindictive man, and she didn't
want to believe he'd be ugly about this.

He leaned forward and looked her straight in the eyes.
"But I don't think he's the right man for you, Emma. You
were young when you married Danny, and the excitement
of being with a fighter jock was great. A real thrill, I'm
sure. But you're not that kid anymore. I know you want a
family. I'm not sure if you're aware, but you've brought
up the subject of fighter pilots a few times. How you were
done with all that flash and burn. That dating a flyboy was
fine for a while, but not for the long term."

She felt her face flush and her anger rise. Had she actually told Gary something so personal? Or had Sharon?
"Wait a minute—"

"I'm not making that up. Sharon was there."

Wow, Emma didn't remember that, which was pretty

messed up. "Even if I did, that's really none of your business."

He looked down, but only for a few seconds. When he met her gaze again, he was full of determination. "I'm sorry if this is uncomfortable, but I take being a friend seriously. And I believe you deserve better. Someone who can offer you stability, who'll be around. Someone you can count on for the long run. Someone patient. Like me."

Emma could barely breathe she was so filled with confusion and, frankly, outrage. "You and Sharon been plotting this talk for a while?"

He shook his head. "No. Although I'm sure she sees the same things I do. I'm not asking you to give up your friendship with Sam. Go for it. Not that I have any say. But you need to know that I'll still be here on the other end."

"The other end of what?"

"Sizzle like that only lasts for so long."

"You do know he's not a fighter pilot any longer. He's an instructor."

Gary nodded. "The job may have changed, but the man was and is a fighter pilot. He'll always be that. Think about the retired pilots we both know. The ones with the speedboats, who do stunt flying in air shows. It's in the blood, Emma."

"Well," she said, gathering her purse and standing. "I appreciate your opinion. I'll certainly keep it under advisement."

"Look, all you really need to know is I'm not going anywhere."

"Okay." She barely managed a token smile. "Thanks for the chai."

"Running tomorrow?"

"We'll see," she said. "I'm having dinner with Sam, and I'm not sure how late I'll be out."

"Either way, I'll be at the track."

She nodded, then left the BX, her anger fueling her quick walk to her car. *Of all the nerve.* Gary had no business shoving his way into her business. No right. They were friends. Colleagues. So she ran with him in the mornings. And they'd palled around outside work sometimes. He didn't get to have an opinion on who she dated or what she did with her private life.

As she made her way out of the base, she had to brake suddenly for a motorcycle. It wasn't the sports model that Sam was interested in, but it stopped her inner rant short.

Okay, so Gary wasn't completely wrong. She couldn't deny that, at least not for long. He'd brought up most of her own arguments and held them in front of her face. But the thought of not seeing Sam tonight made her ache.

What Gary didn't know, what no one could know, including her, was how his nonflight status was going to change Sam's life. He wanted a family. He knew what it was to have an absentee father. One of the things that kept popping up in articles about the new RPA fleet was how it gave active duty pilots an eight-to-five life, which they'd never had when flying the fast movers.

Yes, she and Sam would have to discuss the motorcycle, but she had faith he would see reason. He wasn't a kid anymore, just as she wasn't. They weren't destined to crash and burn. And she wasn't going to bail when they'd barely started.

THE BANKS OF VIDEO SCREENS were spaced just far enough apart that Sam could efficiently keep his focus on one simulator bay at a time in short bursts of intense concentration. He and two other instructors that he barely knew had been assigned their individual sections, and as it was the first day for the trainees to be in the simulators, the instructors had fed in the same practice video, each spooled to run at the same time.

Sam's coffee was growing cold even though he held it in his hand. It would take some getting used to, this arrangement and the screen array. During his own training, things had been just different enough that he'd need to reprogram his movements and find a new rhythm.

"Sandoval better be having first-day jitters." Captain Cooper jiggled the keys in his uniform pocket. An unconscious habit, evidently, and one Sam refused to let under his skin. "Because he's lost tracking on that vehicle three times already."

"I'd give it a week before coming to any conclusions about this batch," Lieutenant Colonel Adams said. He'd been an instructor at Holloman for three years and had a lot of experience, which was why he was in the instructor's bay with Sam and Cooper, who were the new kids in town. "Almost everyone gets a pass before we get down and dirty."

Even though they went through the first phase of instrument simulator flying and academics, the students would be piloting real MQ-9s and using live payloads.

Not today, though. First three days were simulations only. Second through fifth week was tracking with no armaments. The students needed to get their bearings, but more important, the instructors needed those first weeks to get the true measure of their trainees. Not everyone made it through.

Sam's gaze went back to the top row of screens, and while there was some sloppy tracking going on, his section seemed to be doing okay.

Something on middle row right caught his eye. The pilot was an 18X by the name of Second Lieutenant Zachary. The sensor in the next seat over was a former helicopter pilot, Lieutenant Wilson. It was Zachary whom Sam was watching, and the guy was moving lower than recommended and damned if he didn't trigger an arms release. All the students had been given the mission of tracking a specific white SUV through desert terrain. Tracking did not mean blowing shit up, even if it was all pretend.

"Colonel, I've got a problem in simulator bay 4A55."

"Go handle it," Adams said, and Sam left the trailer.

The sun was brutal outside, and the walk was a long one to Zachary's bay. This was the kind of behavior that had to be nipped in the bud, and Sam used the time before he got to 4A55 to go over what he'd need to say.

He surprised the two men, but they didn't stop the mission, which was good, because he would have raised hell if they had. Positioning himself at the back of the crowded simulator bay, Sam crossed his arms, focusing on Zachary, but his sensor would take the heat as if he'd done the deed. "You know why I'm here, gentlemen?"

"Yes, sir," Zachary said. "I stepped outside the mission parameter, sir."

"Yes, you did. And it troubles me, Lieutenant, because every time you put your thumb on a red button, you are prepared to kill. Every time. This is not a video game where you get to try again. Just as with your service weapon, the only time you aim is when you are prepared to end lives. There is no room in this air force for men who treat these RPAs as anything less than the active and dangerous weapons they are. Do you understand, Lieutenant?"

"Yes, sir."

"Lieutenant Wilson, did you go over the mission parameters with your pilot before you put your MQ in the air?"

"Yes, sir."

"Were you aware that Lieutenant Zachary had engaged the armaments?"

"No, sir."

"I suggest you gentlemen reread your regulations, and go over your training materials, because this is the last warning you'll ever receive about misuse and mishandling of an RPA. Are we clear?"

"Yes, sir."

"Carry on," he said, then stepped outside once again. Those two would be on their best behavior, knowing that getting called out on day one was no way to get ahead. And Wilson would probably have plenty to say to his partner. All Sam knew for sure was that he did not want one of his trainees to wash out. In fact, he didn't want to hear of any kind of misconduct, malicious or not, from any member of his team.

Frankly, the whole screwup pissed him off. God, they were young. Sam remembered the kind of stunts he, Danny and John had pulled during their initial training, but never in class, never with the equipment. They'd gotten stupid in bars and cars and, God knew, with women.

But the three of them had understood that when they were in a classroom or a simulator or a plane, it was all business, all the time. His students would learn the same thing before the initial phase of training was over. He'd see to it.

As he headed back to his trailer, he pulled out his cell. Emma would be between classes at the moment. Her schedule was more complicated than half the missions he'd flown, but he'd memorized most of it.

"Hey, Captain," she said, answering on the first ring.

"Got a minute?"

"You bet."

"I just had to give one of my students hell." When she didn't reply, he realized his voice had probably clued her in that he wasn't finished. "It was hard. I didn't like it."

Emma laughed, and he wasn't sure if it was with him or at him. "Oh, sweetie, you really are a rookie teacher. But don't worry, it gets easier."

He was grinning himself. It wasn't the first time he'd had to chew out a subordinate, but he'd still milk the situation for all it was worth. "Ah, so you were laughing at me."

"Completely."

"Fine. Be that way. The thing is, I want my people to want to do well. I want them to fight to be the best. It's my job to motivate them to do exactly that."

"Ah, sweetie, it's your first day. Give it a minute. I can't imagine you being anything less than the best instructor at the base."

"Thank you," he said, making it sound like he was pouting. "I think I deserve to go out for Mexican tonight. How late is your online class?"

Emma cleared her throat, but she couldn't completely hide her laugh behind it. "Wow, if you're going to eat a couple of chimichangas every time you have to dress down a student, you won't be fitting in those tight jeans of yours for long."

"How'd you remember I like those damn things?"

"There's lots I remember about you. And yet I still want to know more."

"I look forward to it." Shit, he had to stop grinning like this while in uniform. "Starting tonight?"

"Dinner still won't work for me, but save room for dessert, will you? Oh, gotta go."

He hung up and slowed his walk, trying to convince his enthusiasm over dessert to settle the hell down so his fellow instructors wouldn't think he got off on chastising students.

12

THE NIGHT WAS WARM, of course, but at the end of September, fall was beginning to sneak in during the evenings. Which made attending Music in the Park at the amphitheater all the better. Of course, just being with Sam was treat enough.

Things were going amazingly well—it was sometimes hard to believe. There were still things to work out. His bachelor habits for one. He was trying to pick up after himself, but his idea of clean and hers were different. It had taken almost two weeks for Emma to realize he actually didn't see clutter the way she did. Seriously, he could walk right past a screwdriver on the mantel a dozen times. She imagined he'd only look for it when he needed the tool again.

The important thing was, he was trying. And she was trying to loosen up. Just because she was overly organized didn't mean he had to follow suit.

Danny certainly hadn't, but that hadn't been why she'd wanted to leave him. In fact, it was very low on the scale of grievances.

Sam, on the other hand, had been crazy good about putting their relationship at the top of his priorities. Okay, it was a tie with his job, but that made perfect sense. If anything, she was the one who sometimes had to bail on dinner or evenings out because of her online class or to lend support to Sharon. The poor woman was an hour away from going into meltdown over her new play, and Sam was incredibly understanding when she had to be gone.

"What's all this thinking about?" he asked, holding out a paper cup of lemonade. "You haven't touched your sandwich."

She smiled at him, his handsome face still setting off the butterflies in her stomach. At times it was a little overwhelming. She would find herself thinking, *I've got the best one. Of all the men ever.* She never said it out loud, but how she felt wasn't exactly a secret.

Taking her drink, she leaned over for a kiss. It took her plate almost slipping from her lap to bring them back to their picnic dinner on the grass, surrounded by half the population of Alamo, or so it seemed. Luckily people were too busy rocking out to one of the local bands to pay much attention.

"I know that smile," he said. "What do you want this time?"

"Excuse me?" Her grin turned to a glare. "What's that supposed to mean?"

"Come on, you can't fool me. I'm onto you." He put his plate down and went from sitting cross-legged to on his knees, hands on his thighs, his gaze unwavering. "You're going to ask me to do something I don't want to do. You're plotting." He pointed one finger at her. "That was the look you had when you took me shirt shopping."

"A man can't live in polo shirts alone, sweetie."

"And when you made me watch that chick flick." He shuddered as if he'd been scarred for life.

"Fine. It wasn't as good as I'd remembered. But you

made me watch that zombie thing. Which was incredibly gross by the way."

"And watching Keanu Reeves be all brokenhearted wasn't?"

"Okay. Point taken. But just because that movie was a bomb doesn't mean we're never watching another romance."

He sighed, then kissed the tip of her nose. "Of course not. Wouldn't dare presume. But I'm not wrong. You are plotting something."

"Well, you know there's music happening soon."

Sam's eyes narrowed. "Hence the name Music in the Park?"

"Sometimes couples, you know, dance."

"Ah. I see your evil plan. And as long as you don't care that people are probably going to point and laugh, I'll be your dancing fool."

She almost lost hold of her dinner in her hurry to hug him, but both sandwich and potato salad were saved. The pickle, alas, was a goner.

He pushed to his feet and took his paper plate to a trash can. She really had been lost in thought for him to have polished off his food without her knowing. But this was good because now she'd get to see his butt twice. He'd take her plate when she was finished. Sam was even more thoughtful than she'd remembered. Or maybe that came with age. Although Danny at thirty had still been the same kid he was at twenty. The thought had barely formed when she put the brakes on. She couldn't think about him. It wasn't fair to compare the two men. They'd both had healthy egos, but Sam had always been more steady.

She was, however, awfully impressed with how he was handling his teaching duties. He took it very seriously, as if every single trainee was not just a student, but his personal responsibility. He'd stay late if needed, but he was strict as hell if one of his pupils stepped out of line.

Once, when she was straightening his desk filing system, she'd gotten a look at his work notes. He might not have gotten to know their first names that initial week, but it was clear he'd homed in on their strengths and weaknesses, and approached the problems with real insight. Whether he believed it or not, he was a born teacher. She should know.

Just as he was settling back next to her, a roar seemed to fill the bowl of the theater. At first, she thought planes, because there were always planes, but nope, this was different. She turned to look over her shoulder.

"Hogs," Sam said, his eyes lighting up.

"You mean Harleys."

"I do. Lots of them, from the sound of it."

Emma studied her sandwich for a few seconds debating, then turned to Sam. "Have you given any more thought to that bike you were so interested in?"

He blinked at her, mouth slightly parted, brow creased. "You know, I haven't. Not at all."

Inside, Emma breathed a huge sigh of relief, but on the outside, she didn't even smile. "Really?"

"Nope. Between hanging out with you and the job, the idea kind of got lost."

"Huh. An adrenaline junky like you? I would have thought—"

Sam leaned sideways until they bumped shoulders. "No motorcycle could possibly rev my engine the way you do, babe."

Her laugh was louder than she'd meant it to be, but maybe that was because she didn't want him to see how grateful she was to hear those words. And twice as grateful to believe them.

AT LEAST HE WASN'T the only man without a hint of rhythm pretending to dance on the grass as the band played an unintelligible song. Emma, on the other hand, made it difficult not to throw her over his shoulder and take her somewhere more private to ravage her until they both couldn't breathe.

This was his life. Loud and messy and filled with joys he'd never dreamed of. Mostly in the form of his Emma, but just as strangely, he wasn't hating his job. In fact, there was a certain satisfaction to guiding those eager trainees to serve their country using all this new tech. The variety of students was interesting, especially with the friction between the old-time cockpit pilots and the new era of straight-to-RPA pilots. He was dead center in the middle of a sea change in the military. Before his twenty was up, the number of drone pilots would dwarf the active flyers, at least when it came to fighting jets. They'd still need transport and cargo planes as long as there were troops on the ground, but he could envision a time when there were few all-manned aircraft units.

He'd have given anything to have had more time in a cockpit, but this job was just as important.

Emma grabbed his waist and tried to get him to move to her beat, but yeah, that probably wasn't going to happen. God knew he was a freak for music, as anyone who dared touch his vinyl would attest, but the dancing thing? Next life, maybe.

Didn't mean he couldn't laugh and enjoy her efforts. Jeez, she made him happy. It was hard to believe that he truly hadn't given a thought to the Hayabusa since he'd been to the dealership. He'd started a downward spiral at the time, so certain life had dealt him a crippling blow. He'd had a year to adjust to being grounded while he was in training to be an instructor. But coming to Holloman had required him to face reality without pity or blinders.

And then there was Emma…. Man, he'd really figured he'd blown it with her that first night at dinner. How many times had he kicked himself for blurting out that he was grounded? He could've waited, or cushioned the news by telling her about a possible correction. Not that he was overly hopeful about the experimental surgery. He barely liked to think about it lest he become too invested in the idea of being fixed. The waiting list was long and even if he was selected, there was no guarantee the surgery would correct his vision enough to fly again.

Although if he *could* qualify to fly again, wouldn't that just be the icing on the cake? But no, he wasn't greedy. He had so much already. And even though he knew Emma was disappointed that he wasn't flying a Raptor, she'd never said one word. Which just proved that he was the luckiest son of a bitch on the planet.

Music and crowd be damned, Sam pulled her into his arms and kissed her until the song…and the next…ended.

"FOR THE RECORD, I hate Shakespeare. I hate acting students. I hate costumes. I hate scenery. But most of all, I hate that every year I volunteer to participate in these nightmare plays, and that I never learn."

Emma patted Sharon on the back, and in the true spirit of friendship, offered her the last chocolate chip cookie.

Sharon shook her head. "Thanks. But when I realized I couldn't call in sick with no chance of recovery I brought the hard stuff."

"No, you didn't," Emma said, opening up Sharon's tote bag. It said something about how dire things were that Sharon didn't even try to stop her. Emma pulled out a jar of Marshmallow Fluff and a tablespoon. Of course she thought of Sam and his stupid fluffernutter sandwiches. Though it took so little to send her mind in his direction. "I'm not letting you eat this."

"I became an adult so I could eat what I wanted, when I wanted to. So yes. I am."

"My God," Gary said as he entered the break room. "You don't even have to try to visualize that stuff clogging your arteries."

"Shut up," Sharon said, then turned to point at Irene and Gail, two of the math teachers who were mostly trying to ignore the fuss to concentrate on their lunches. "Don't judge me. I've had four salads this week. Four."

Emma's attention was stuck on Gary. It had been over two weeks since they'd had that discussion in the café, and although he hadn't brought up the topic of Sam since then, she hadn't truly relaxed.

The urge at the moment was to tell him about the bike. How Sam hadn't given it another thought, but bringing it up seemed…childish. She had nothing to prove to Gary. He had a right to think whatever he wanted about her relationship as long as he kept it to himself. And anyway, why should she care what he thought?

But she did. She wanted things to be the way they were before that stupid run up to Cloudcroft. Everything else had been obviously friend-based with a hint of maybe on the side. The picnic, though, despite her treating it like a race instead of a run, had been different.

"I'll share my turkey sandwich with you," he said, sitting down next to Sharon at the round table. "And if you still want your goop after, be my guest."

Sharon gave him a look that should have singed his eyebrows. "Well, gee, Gary, now that I have your permission, I feel so much better." She took the jar and opened it. Her dramatic gesture was somewhat diluted by the trouble she had removing the safety seal, but then she took a big old spoonful and stuck it straight in her mouth.

Gary looked pleadingly at Emma, who backed away from the table. It was the move of a chicken, but there was no way she was getting in the middle of that mess.

"Fine," he said. "I give up. I will forever stay out of any discussion about your food choices."

"That's good," Sharon said. "Because Joe and I are having a barbecue next Sunday, after the stupid play is over forever, and I want you to make your ribs."

"You brazen wench," he said. "You've got some nerve."

"I know. I'm completely unpredictable. But you'll still come, yes?"

"Yes."

Sharon pointed her spoon at Emma. "I'd like you to bring salad and lemonade. Does Sam have any specialties?"

Emma darted a look at Gary, but he was digging into his turkey sandwich, seemingly without a care. "He used to do burgers and stuff on the roof of our apartment building. And he's great at buying beer."

"All right, then burgers and beer it is." Sharon turned to Gary again. "Okay with you?"

"He'll feel bad when everybody eats all my ribs and his burgers are left to burn in ignominy."

"Ignominy?" Emma said. "Did someone have a special word of the day on their calendar this morning?"

"Mock me if you will, but I stand by my choice. Now pass me the thingy that makes salt dust."

She laughed. He was funny, always had been. But there was still no comparison to Sam. It wasn't Sam's hotshot credentials that set him apart. He'd grown into such a fine man. She could go on for ages about his thoughtfulness, how he went out of his way not only for his students, but for her. He always made sure to have dinner ready if she had to work late. Mostly he got takeout, but she had no problem with that. On nights they were both home, they shared the task equally.

He might not be the neatest kid on the block, but he put his laundry in the hamper and didn't give her any grief about wanting the kitchen in a particular order. On her league nights, he took care of his washing and ironing so they wouldn't get in each other's way. He hadn't been back to bowling. They'd agreed it was probably for the best, considering.

But it was time for him to get to know her friends better, meet some he hadn't met yet, and good for Sharon for breaching the subject so well. Emma didn't want to hide him. Although since they'd decided to be together, she hadn't wanted to share him much.

Tonight, it was Sam who would be home late. A meeting of instructors with some bigwig from D.C. coming to talk about the RPA program. The need for pilots and sensors had outpaced all expectations. Holloman trained almost four hundred pilot pairs per session, but there were rumors they might go to two shifts.

Sam had already told her he'd do all he could to keep to his schedule. Eight to five, five days a week. Just like real people. Nothing like a fighter pilot.

When Danny had been flying, he worked a ton of twelve-hour shifts, got deployed six months out of every two years, and on top of that, was assigned temporary duty three or four times a year, so it seemed almost unbelievable that Sam had gotten so lucky. It felt almost too good to be true.

If she had any complaint at all it was the bouncing back

and forth part. They'd spent every night together, half the time at her house, the other half at his apartment. Sam had mentioned that it was crazy to keep two places, and though she agreed, they hadn't explored the topic of moving in together. They'd sort of just let it fade. She couldn't recall why. A lot of things seemed to fall by the wayside when they'd started kissing and making out like sixteen-year-olds. That was why she refused to grocery shop with him. She didn't trust either of them not to cause a scene.

If this chemistry between them played out like she was hoping, they'd have the perfect life, really. Not that she'd ever admit it, but sometimes she let herself think about a long-term life with Sam. He'd admitted he wanted kids, so did she. At least two were on the wish list she'd brought out of storage and dusted off. With his reasonable hours, he'd have time to help with their kids' homework. Time to go to soccer practice, to take his daughter to ballet.

She knew she was jumping the gun. It had only been a few weeks, not nearly long enough to tell if they were meant for marriage and family. Sure, they'd known each other forever, but it would be foolish to ignore that they each had changed some. Despite the fact that Sam said he'd forgotten about that motorcycle, she didn't allow herself that luxury.

Her gaze went back to Gary. She thought of how certain he'd sounded, as if it was a foregone conclusion that Sam would revert to type. But Gary didn't seem to realize that there were all kinds of fighter pilots. Including those who wanted a more traditional life. Good thing she'd remembered herself before she'd discounted Sam.

She ended up eating her cookie, listening to Sharon and Gary bicker like an old married couple. Emma would never admit it, and even thinking about it made her feel guilty, but she was glad Sam couldn't fly anymore. That the choice had been taken out of his hands. God bless the air force and their rigid rules. Nothing short of a miracle would put Sam in a cockpit again.

13

EMMA KICKED SAM's front door shut behind her, seeing as how she'd had to juggle keys, purse, laptop and briefcase. Naturally, that was when her phone rang.

She managed to fetch her cell, smiling the second she saw it was Sam. "Hello, gorgeous," she said.

"It's my turn to make dinner."

Her view to the kitchen was unimpaired and the only things missing from it were Sam and dinner. "I imagine you're slaving away at the stove right now."

The door from the garage opened and Sam came in carrying a bag from the Golden Dragon. His grin was completely unapologetic. "It felt like a Chinese kind of night."

"If you saw me struggling at the door while you drove by and decided to prank call instead of helping me, I'll have to hurt you."

He put the bag on the dividing counter, his phone in his pocket and pulled her close. "I would never do that."

"Good answer."

"Shall I set the table?" He found that sensitive spot on the side of her neck. "Or is there something else you'd rather we do?"

She grinned, kissed him, but instead of lingering like

she wanted to, she said, "Oh, there's something else, all right, but you won't like it. I need to put away my things, and then get my laundry started before we eat."

He frowned. "Seriously? Laundry wins over me making mad passionate love to you?" When she giggled, he lowered his head as he looked up because he knew what those puppy dog eyes did to her. "I got you your favorite."

It probably would have been more of an enticement to eat now if he didn't always get her favorite. "Thank you, that's very sweet. But my things still need putting away, and I have to either wash clothes or drive to my house before tomorrow morning."

"No, we don't want that," he said, releasing her and then squeezing her butt as he passed. It was one of his favorite things to do. Well, that and surprise her with sneaky kisses. "How about I start a load while you're putting away your stuff?"

"After you change, you can start the washer—that would help." She ignored his smile. So she was particular about how she washed and dried her clothes. He was careful with his uniforms, therefore, they were even.

She watched him walk toward the bedroom, then turned to the briefcase she'd set down on the floor. Her gaze fell on the kitchen trash bin. Poking out from under this morning's napkins was a brochure. Something about it compelled her to pull it free. Her heart lurched in her chest as she realized what it was: a sales brochure for the sports bike. The peregrine falcon on wheels.

Just looking at the sleek, aerodynamic motorcycle made her cringe at how fast it was capable of going. How she'd have worried for his life every day if he'd bought it, even if they'd never become lovers.

That he'd thrown it in the trash was amazing. She felt certain he hadn't left it there for her to see. He didn't know how she felt about the stupid thing because she hadn't said. He'd tossed it because it no longer called to him.

Maybe it was because he liked being an instructor more than he'd ever imagined. Or perhaps it was because they'd been so busy together that he didn't have time to think about the bike. But it was also quite possible that he'd done it for her. For them.

Emma found him coming out of the bedroom, his uniform replaced by her favorite worn jeans and a tight-fitting white T-shirt. Before he even knew what hit him, she was climbing him like a tree, her hands in his hair, her kiss leaving no questions about what they were going to do for dessert.

Being a man of action, he helped by cupping her bottom as she kept trying to wrap her leg around his hips, holding them both steady with his other hand and giving as good as he got in the kiss department.

She considered dragging him straight into the bedroom, but no, this was enough for now. She could feel his enthusiasm getting harder by the moment and his moans were of the oh-God-don't-stop variety.

But they did have to breathe. He pulled back first, clearly puzzled. "Why?"

She smiled as she moved in for a second round. "Because I'm crazy in love with…moo shoo pork."

It wasn't a big surprise that Sam insisted on helping her with the laundry. Or that he sneaked in a couple of his own items. Standing shoulder to shoulder in the garage laundry alcove they made sure pockets were emptied and her delicates were in the lingerie bag. He'd left a tag on one of his camo shirts, but in the end, the first load, the one without towels, was full enough and Emma bent over to start the machine.

She'd expected a grope, but Sam's phone rang, and when he looked at the caller's name, his back straightened and his brows went up. He walked away from the rumble of the washer to say hello.

She thought about waiting for him but that seemed intrusive. Most likely it was someone from work, but it could have been his mom or John. Maybe even someone from his old base.

Anyway, it was time for her to start sorting out their dinner. She left him leaning against his Mustang as she walked back into the house. His "Are you serious?" something to intrigue her as she got out plates and chopsticks and the most adorable handmade soy sauce bowls she'd gotten at the Fall Festival the year before.

He'd probably want a beer, but she didn't take it out in case this was a soda night. She broke with tradition and poured herself a ginger ale. Then she portioned out their plates, him with the lion's share of lo mein, and her hogging most of the moo shoo.

She did keep glancing at the garage door. Before dinner was over she wanted to tell him about the barbecue at Sharon's, and see if he felt comfortable enough to come. God, she hoped—

"You are never going to believe this," he said, slamming through the door. His eyes were wide and his cheeks flushed, and her heart started pumping fast.

"What?"

"It was the surgeon's office from California. Someone dropped out of the program, and they want me to take her place. Shit. They'd said it would be a year, maybe two."

A surgeon from California? "What are you talking about?" She crossed her arms over her T-shirt and stood still with her hip against the counter. Someone had to counterbalance Sam practically flying around the room.

"You know about the screwup with my left eye."

"Uh-huh."

He shook his head, and she could tell he was trying to calm down so he could explain. "There's a chance it can be fixed. I probably won't get to 20/20, but hey…" He looked at his watch. "I can still teach class tomorrow, then fly to Los Angeles in the evening. Basically I'll only miss one day of work."

"Whoa. Slow down."

"What?" He stared at her as if he was having trouble focusing. "Emma, this is amazing. I didn't expect this."

Obviously neither had she, since she had no idea what he was talking about.

"I'll fly commercial," he said, mostly to himself. "I can't afford to hop a transport and miss the appointment."

"Wait— You've already confirmed you're going?"

"Well, yeah. I turn down this chance and I'm back on the list, and it literally could take another year."

"What list?"

He stared at her for a moment. "I'm sorry, honey. I forgot you don't know the details." He breathed in deeply, then moved closer to take her hand. "The complication I had only affects a small percentage of people, yet it's enough for doctors to work on a fix because the surgery itself has uses outside of this particular issue. They've been at it for several years and their success rate is impressive."

"Is it laser surgery? You know stats?"

"Yes." He smiled and rubbed her arm. "A few years ago they were able to help one out of five people. Now the success rate is significantly better."

"Okay," she said, the information trickling into her brain in bits and pieces. She'd never had a problem with her vision, but she could understand wanting to see clearly without contacts or glasses. "Can you just leave tomorrow evening?"

He nodded. "Colonel Stevens knows I'm on the wait list. He won't have a problem with me going. It's a huge opportunity."

Emma tensed. His boss knew? So why hadn't Sam told her? And why would he tell his boss something like that, anyway? A horrible thought occurred to her. No, this surgery couldn't be about qualifying to fly again. The air force was strict about vision requirements. "You never mentioned... I had no idea this was even a possibility."

"Not because I didn't want you to know." His hand moved up her arm to massage the tightness in her shoulder. "I didn't like thinking about it. This procedure isn't regularly scheduled. I've been on the list for six months and was told it would be another year, minimum, so I wasn't counting on anything happening this soon."

"Tell me this isn't experimental." Her tone came out all wrong. He was excited, and he hadn't mentioned anything about flying. She was probably worried for nothing...

"Not the way you're thinking. The only reason I'm eligible is because there's something unique about the curvature of my cornea."

He pulled her arms around his waist so he could hold her close. "I can't believe this."

"Me, neither."

"I have to call the colonel. I'd like to give him as much notice as possible."

"Of course."

He leaned back to look at her. "What's the matter?"

She shrugged, not wanting to rain all over his joy. She even managed a weak smile. "I think I'm still in shock."

"I wish I'd thought to tell you. I just...I don't know... didn't want to get your hopes up, I guess."

"*My* hopes up? Your eye is basically healthy, right? Even if you didn't have this new surgery."

"Oh, yeah, don't worry about that. I couldn't be teaching if it wasn't. No, this is only about qualifying to fly."

Her heart sank. Though she hadn't needed to hear him say the words. On some level she'd understood the surgery, his excitement—it was all about being able to fly. She couldn't admit she liked the way things were. Exactly how they were…seeing each other every night, eating dinner together, talking about their days. Flying would change everything. "What about the risks? Did they tell you what they are?"

"Risks? Oh, no. Not this time. The worst that could happen is that I still wouldn't qualify. That's it."

"Sam, it's a laser in your eye. Of course there are risks."

He stepped back. Away. "Okay, technically, you're right. There are risks. But with this surgery, they're minimal. Like less than two percent."

"And what happened to the two percent?"

"Their vision got worse. Not dramatically. But for me, it wouldn't matter, because anything below regulation and I'm screwed, so…"

Wow. He was going to go for it. Regardless. Although he was looking at her again with concern.

"Are you saying you don't want me to do this?" he asked, his eyes narrowing.

"I would never tell you that. It's your decision. But you have to realize, all this is completely new information. It's a lot to take in."

"I'm not going in half-cocked. I learned my lesson the first time around."

Had he really? Sam was a risk-taker. What he deemed acceptable, most people wouldn't. Including her. She turned to the microwave so he couldn't see her face, and tried to figure out how long to heat his dinner. It was no use. Her concentration was shot. She made a wild guess and hoped the food didn't burn. "I wouldn't mind knowing more of the details."

Sam nodded. "I get that, but seriously, there's nothing to worry about. Would you like to come with me? Would that help?"

His not having already made up his mind was what would've helped. "I really can't, not with pop quizzes this week." She looked over her shoulder at him. "Unless you think you might need me."

"I'll always need you, Emma." He came up behind her and circled his arms around her waist, bent his head to kiss the side of her neck. "Always."

Her heart caught. Danny had once said similar words that had proved untrue. Different men, she reminded herself. Very different for all they had in common. Still, she felt horrible for how subdued Sam had become when he'd been over the moon minutes ago. She leaned against his chest and clung to his forearms. "You hungry?"

"I will be."

She watched the seconds tick away, the microwave turntable spinning like her thoughts. His enthusiasm shouldn't have surprised her. He was a pilot. He'd never claimed to be anything but. It'd been hell for him to be banned from the cockpit, and she'd felt guilty for being glad of it.

But her perfect little bubble had burst, just as his dream looked to be coming true.

Gary had been right.

Maybe she was overreacting. The news had come out of the blue. The only thing she had to do right now was support him. It was no use pretending that she wasn't in love with him. That she'd crossed a line only to find it had been the edge of the world. And she refused to let her own selfish wishes play a part in his decision. She wasn't going to be that woman.

If that meant that they couldn't be together in the end…? No, she wasn't going to do that to herself. He wasn't Danny. Sam had already shown her that he could be considerate and thoughtful about his safety and their relationship.

"Honey?"

She turned to see him frowning.

"I really did learn my lesson when I had the first surgery. All I'd wanted was to never have to bother with contact lenses or glasses again. It never occurred to me that I could lose so much. With this procedure, though, the risk is so minuscule it's barely statistically meaningful."

Two percent wasn't minuscule. Especially when it came to someone's eyesight. But Sam was smart. He knew that, and she wasn't about to argue because clearly he'd made up his mind.

"There's a slight chance I'd have to use eyedrops," he continued. "A slight chance my vision won't improve, or could get a little worse. We're only talking about my left eye, and the reason I was chosen is because they believe the outcome will be favorable."

He turned her to face him and touched her cheek. "Please don't be worried. It's an acceptable level of risk. I swear."

She smiled, doing her damndest to make it as real as possible. "I want the best for you, Sam. In every way. I want you safe and I want you happy."

"I know that. And I understand it's scary. You haven't had any time to process what's happening but unfortunately this is a take-it-or-lose-it situation. So, are we okay?"

She kissed him, because she hadn't been lying. She did want him happy. She just hoped they would end up happy together.

LUCKILY, COLONEL STEVENS was at home, and didn't mind speaking to Sam even though he was eating dinner. He went over the particulars, making sure that Stevens knew the plan was to miss the least amount of time.

Even though he was pacing, Sam made sure the entire conversation was transparent to Emma. He wished he'd thought to mention the surgery when he'd first told her about his eyes, but he couldn't help that now. That she was so worried bothered him, and he wasn't exactly sure how to make it better.

Truth was, if their positions had been reversed, he'd have felt the same.

"I believe there's a transport plane heading to San Francisco tomorrow at five, if that would help."

"I'll check into that, sir. Thank you. I'm perfectly fine with taking commercial flights, but my first call tomorrow will be to Manpower and Personnel."

"For the record, if all this works out I'd rather you stayed here with us in the RPA program, but I know your old CO. He wasn't planning on losing you, and those cockpit seats are becoming rarer and rarer. Who knows, maybe we can keep you on board at Holloman. It would mean training on a Raptor."

"I'd be honored to fly a Raptor, sir. It would mean a lot just to be considered. But first, I have to get over this hurdle, make sure my eyes are air force ready." His gaze slid to Emma, to see her reaction to the possibility, but instead of smiling, she looked even more tense. He turned away so he didn't lose the thread with his atypically chatty superior. Perhaps the man had had a drink before his meal.

The colonel cleared his throat, and his "Good luck with that, Captain" ended his part in the conversation.

"Thank you, sir." Sam hung up, but didn't put down his phone. He wanted to go talk to Emma, but his window for getting out to L.A. was tight as hell. What he did do was join her at the counter, where her moo shoo pork was getting colder by the minute. "I have to make a couple of calls," he said, "but why don't you go ahead and eat?"

She looked at her plate as if she'd forgotten it was there. "Okay."

"Are you sure you don't want to come with me? It's just as easy to get flights for two."

"I would if I could, but it would be really tricky with my class schedule. Besides, you'll only be gone overnight."

He kissed her, aching to comfort her, but there was so much to gain if this surgery worked out, he didn't dare pass up the opportunity. "I'll be done as soon as I can."

She squeezed his arm, and went back to staring into the microwave.

His first call was over fast. There was a transport going to California, but it was at the wrong time. He had some wiggle room, since he'd fly tomorrow evening and his appointment wasn't until early the following morning. But he wasn't willing to cut it too close. It took a while and a lot of pacing to get through to a person instead of a computer at the airline, but once he did, they worked out the fastest, most direct flights.

He'd land at the Burbank airport, stay at a nearby motel, then take a cab to his surgeon's office in the morning. That same afternoon he'd fly back home. That he'd be released so quickly after the surgery should've reassured Emma. No, the information hadn't helped. She still seemed tense.

After he made a hotel reservation and was finally able to put his cell in the charger, he went directly into his office and grabbed the file he'd kept on the original procedure and the potential fix. When he returned to Emma, she was still standing in the kitchen. It smelled like Chinese food, but there were no plates on the table. Somewhere during his conversation with the airline, he'd heard the washing machine buzzer go off. It didn't matter, not when it was so clear Emma was not okay. What he couldn't figure out was why.

This could mean so much to them. Not that being an instructor wasn't important and better than he'd imagined, but it wasn't flying. Not ass in the seat, Mach 2, do it or die flying.

More than ever, he wanted to be at the top of his game. He wanted Emma to be proud of him, to know he was an elite fighter, a modern-day warrior who wasn't afraid to face the front lines.

Her gaze went straight to the folder, and okay, okay, she wasn't thinking that far ahead. All this was because she was worried that something could go wrong.

That, he could handle. They could handle. While she looked through the paperwork, he stood right by her, going over all the material, explaining each step. He took it slow, and as it went on, especially the part where it talked about their specific success with his exact curvature issue, Emma's body relaxed until she was leaning more against him than the counter.

"Feel better?"

She hesitated. "Better, yes. But I won't be happy until you're home."

He kissed her, as tenderly as he knew how. He'd had lovers and he'd had girlfriends, but he'd never had anyone like Emma. The worry in her expression was both troubling and humbling. He wanted to ease her mind, and the quickest way he knew how to do that was to get out to California and come back ASAP.

"You should eat," he said.

"So should you. And I need to transfer the clothes to the dryer."

He nodded, but he didn't move. "How about we put all that stuff on hold. Say, an hour?"

Her smile wasn't a full-on heart-stopper, but it was real. "What did you have in mind, Captain?"

A kiss on her nose as he threaded his fingers between hers was followed by a very awkward walk to the bedroom. He kept stopping to kiss some other part, which tended to trip them up.

It was worth it, though, to nibble on her ear, to lick a stripe up her neck until he could feel her pulse beneath his tongue.

By the time they reached the door, his Emma was back. Her hands were underneath his T-shirt, until he bumped into the side of the bed.

"I know you're trying to distract me," she said.

"How am I doing?"

She stripped off her own shirt and dropped it on the floor. "Really well."

14

HE'D SAID THINGS had gone well.

That was what Emma should have been concentrating on. No, actually, she should have been keeping an eye on her students as they took their exam instead of staring at the cell phone in her lap. Not wondering what exactly Sam meant by *gone well.*

Of course he'd say things had *gone well,* right? Even if he'd lost all vision in his left eye, he wasn't about to tell her from eight hundred miles away. Or by voice mail.

But he'd sounded good. Admitted things were fuzzy for now, and then he'd had to go. The second message had been much like the first, except he'd said everything was fine.

Fine. She'd never cared much for that word, either. Fine was what you said when you didn't want to tell the truth.

Damn time and damn travel, and now he wasn't even flying on a commercial flight where there would be a slight window for him to call her back.

Of course her phone was on vibrate, and she couldn't have walked out of class. Unless it was an emergency, but he hadn't called and wouldn't call again until he was home, and even then, he'd said he was going to try to catch some sleep on the plane.

If only she'd heard him live instead of in voice mails.

She hadn't been this nervous since... Who the hell could remember something stupid like that when all she wanted to do was see Sam?

If she had needed proof that she was in love with the man, today would have sealed the deal. She hadn't been able to eat or sleep since he left, although she'd drunk her weight in coffee.

The flight from Burbank was three hours. The second flight from El Paso, one. He'd been in the air two hours total. She assumed. Because the second flight was a favor, a major landing at the base. The major wasn't someone Sam knew. Any number of things could have knocked the timeline sideways.

The timer went off, and she nearly jumped out of her skin. Luckily, no one was looking up. A collective sigh was heard across the classroom as pens were put down. The shuffle of paper and murmured complaints was somewhat soothing. Now, if only she didn't have office hours.

Maybe no one would show up. That would be worse, actually, to sit there and wait with nothing to distract her. She should call him. It wasn't a big deal.

"Ms. Lockwood?" Caleb Innes stood in front of her desk, although he wasn't looking at her. Instead, he was staring at his notebook edge as he attempted to peel the top layer free.

"Yes?"

"Do you have any extra-credit stuff? To help with my grade?"

"Didn't do so well on the exam, hmm?"

He shook his head, met her gaze for a quarter of a second, which was progress, she supposed.

"Was it the material or did something get in the way of you studying?"

He winced. "I got stuck on a double-double shift. I tried to read my textbook, but it didn't work out."

A lot of her students worked full-time, and some of them more than one job. Caleb was a good student normally. Painfully shy, so he didn't participate much, but he tried. She'd seen the circles under his eyes get darker with each class. "Next week, my office hours, you can try again, okay?"

His shoulders came down and he almost smiled. "Thanks. A lot."

She hoped it worked out for him. He was planning to move on to a four-year degree. He wanted to work with animals.

The phone hadn't magically vibrated without her feeling it, and she only had time to grab a quick coffee before office hours.

By the time she made it there, she'd lost her battle to just put up an apology sign and leave. So she sat, worrying, staring, watching time trickle down like the last bit of ketchup in a bottle.

A knock on the door made her gasp, and before she could say "Come in," Sharon entered. "Will you please tell me what is going on with you today? I'm not kidding, I'm actually worried. Is it some medical thing you're waiting to hear back on?"

Emma hadn't wanted to bring Sharon into the discussion. First of all, it wasn't Emma's thing to share. Although Sharon was her closest friend, and that was what best friends were for. "In a way."

"Oh, God," Sharon said. "One second." She opened the door, turned the small wooden in-session sign over so no one would knock, then sat across from Emma. "Talk to me."

"It's Sam."

Sharon's eyes widened. "Come on. No."

Emma shook her head. "He's having some work done on his left eye."

"Has it gotten worse?"

"No. This is corrective surgery. He's just under regulation, but he's pretty sure this new procedure can fix it."

"Wait. I was all prepared to hear terrible news and be the kind of friend who would be there for you no matter what. I have to adjust a minute."

"So now you're not going to be there for me?"

"Shh. I'm serious. Give me a minute."

Emma didn't want to give her any such thing. He wouldn't be home yet. She'd purposely asked him to go straight to her place so she could be there before him, make something comforting for dinner. In other words, occupy herself, but the flaw was apparent now. Her imagination would still be working overtime. Dammit.

"Is he having the surgery right now?" Sharon asked, serious again.

"Nope. It was this morning. He's on his way home."

"Driving already?"

Emma sighed and glanced at her watch. "He had to go to L.A. He's in the air now."

"Did you speak to him after it was done?"

"Two voice mails. According to him it went well and he's fine."

"But you need to see for yourself."

Emma raised both hands and said, "Exactly," far too loudly. And enthusiastically.

"Question." Sharon adjusted her hair clip, then put on her serious face. "How long have you known about the procedure?"

"Night before last. Before that, I had no idea a fix was even possible."

"Ah." Sharon nodded too slowly for it to be anything but a dramatic effect.

"What?"

"Nothing...just, how do you feel about it?"

"I want him to be healthy."

"Of course you do. We're not talking about that right now, though. If the surgery works, I'm assuming he'll be able to fly again," she said, watching Emma closely as she nodded. "How do you feel about that?"

"Fine." Emma shrugged, not anxious to meet her friend's eyes. "I know I said I was done with pilots," she murmured quietly. "But if flying is what Sam wants to do, then I'm okay with that. I mean, there's no guarantee that even if he does meet the regulations he can transfer. They need drone instructors a lot more than they need fighter pilots."

God help her, she sounded defensive and pitiful. Her stomach was the problem; it wouldn't settle down. She glanced at her watch. Could time possibly drag by any slower?

"You know what?" Sharon stood up. "Go home. None of that matters. Meet him at the door. Smooch the hell out of him."

"I can't. I might have—"

"The students can find you if they need to. Go. Home. Put on your favorite music. Wear something sexy."

"Sharon."

"I mean it," she said, lowering her voice. "It's going to be all right, Em."

"You think?"

"Yeah. Just drive carefully. I'll see you tomorrow."

Emma got her purse, but she still kept her cell in her hand.

THE MUSIC SHE CHOSE was Prokofiev. Bouncy and happy and full of surprises. It lasted five minutes. Next, she decided to go for a classic instead. *Thriller.* Loud enough to piss off her neighbor, who wasn't home, thank goodness, because she needed to be moonwalking across her kitchen floor and singing at the top of her lungs that Billie Jean wasn't her lover as she prepared dinner.

She'd chosen the meal based entirely on two things: Sam's favorite food and what she had in the house. Sadly, since she didn't have baby back ribs, pot roast, porterhouse steaks or homemade pizza, he was getting lasagna. Sort of.

It was a shame she didn't have time to make her special spaghetti sauce, but if she put the jar in the recycle bin, no one would know once she added a shot of cabernet sauvignon. Adding layers of semidefrosted beef ravioli, mozzarella cheese and a generous coating of parmigiano at the end, her wink-and-it's-lasagna was in the oven ten minutes before Sam was scheduled to land at Holloman.

She'd put candles on the table, used her good dishes and the linen napkins. By the time she started putting together a salad, her hands had begun shaking. Enough that she wondered if she should be handling a knife. It was crazy. He was fine. She knew that. She should be more concerned about having the vinaigrette dressing ready before he came home.

As she'd done at the completion of each task, she checked her cell as she put the cruet on the table. No call. No word. Nothing.

Foolish to worry now, though. Right? The surgery was long over. The doctor had released him to come home. And he'd have been back much later if he'd had to fly commercially from El Paso to the dinky airport in Alamo. She shouldn't complain. Or make herself sick waiting.

There was nothing left but to take a shower and get dressed. It would be her second of the day, but she didn't mind. She could continue singing, for one thing, and she wanted to smell good. For Sam.

As she turned on the water and stripped off her clothes, the music wasn't loud enough to stop her from thinking about her answer to Sharon's question.

The truth was, although nothing mattered more to her than Sam being okay, his being a fighter pilot wasn't her first choice. Or even her second.

It would mean no more eight-to-five life. Having kids would become a very different proposition. Not that he wouldn't want to be a good father...he would, but he wouldn't be there a lot. Even if he didn't go overseas, his schedule would be a nightmare, and she'd be on her own a lot of the time.

She stepped under the spray and let it wash away at least some of her worries. There was no need to borrow trouble. She wanted him home. In her arms. Healthy with no complications. Nothing else mattered today. Tomorrow would take care of itself.

The shower didn't last long. She'd taken the precaution of putting the cell's ringer on, and it was sitting within arm's length, but there was no call.

As for putting on something sexy, all she could decide on at the moment was the matching panties and thong he liked so much. In the end, she decided to ditch the underwear and go commando under a sundress. He was a guy. He'd love it.

Then it was waiting. Again. The music stopped and she didn't bother putting on anything else. The food filled the kitchen with the great scent of Italian spices, and her stomach was tied in knots. She sipped her way through half a glass of wine while staring at the clock. He should've landed already. So why hadn't he called? Maybe he misunderstood that she wanted him to call as soon as he landed. She pressed speed dial.

A key unlocked the front door. His key.

Emma ran to meet him and he didn't even have time to put down his duffel bag before she was in his arms. "Why didn't you call me?" she asked, clinging to him, finding comfort in the feel of his warm flesh.

He dropped his bag. "Honey, hold on, I'm here, I'm sorry. My battery ran down because I kept it on all night in case you called, but I'm fine. I swear, just give me a second."

She backed up, although letting go of him completely was out of the question. She needed the reassurance that he was right here and safe with her.

A sudden realization slammed into her. Waiting had been hell. She rarely felt that level of anxiety, and it was only partly to do with the surgery. She'd been afraid he wouldn't come home. Just like Danny hadn't.

A sob caught in her throat. Her reaction was so obvious. Why hadn't she seen it? Sam apparently hadn't, either, and he couldn't know. He assumed this was about his eyes, and she had to keep it that way. "Those aren't your sunglasses. What are they for? Are your eyes all right? May I see them?"

Sam pulled off the big weird sunglasses, but there wasn't much difference. Just a little redness.

"Oh." She managed a smile. "Not so bad."

He drew his thumb across her cheek, and she had the bad feeling a tear had slipped. "I hate that you worried so much. I honestly thought I'd explained sufficiently to avoid that. I'm so sorry."

"I'm fine, really. It's just…you know, I had to see for myself. That's all."

"I do know." He smiled at her. "You're a sight for sore eyes."

That eased the tension. She moaned at the joke, then it occurred to her— "Are they sore?"

"No. Not—" The kitchen timer went off. "It smells great in here. Is that dinner?"

She nodded.

"I'm starving. I've had two protein bars and some terrible coffee all day."

Grateful for the distraction, she left him to turn off the timer. She took a few seconds to slip on oven mitts while her pulse slowed. Sam was here. He was all right. She had nothing more to worry about. At least for tonight. She turned to get the casserole dish out of the oven, but his hand stopped her.

"What I need far more than food is a kiss. And to tell you again that I'm so sorry I made you worry for a minute. It was an insane day, most of it spent waiting in inconvenient places. I did mean to call you more. I simply couldn't."

She went into his arms and did as he asked, so grateful to feel him hug her tight, to taste him, even smell the soft hint of airplane fuel that would need to be washed off before bed.

"I'm glad to be home," he said as he pulled back to look into her eyes. "I promise I'll give you the whole lowdown. But know the doctor was thrilled. It really was a minor surgery, over in five minutes. It won't take long at all to heal. I'll have to go back in a week, but only for an afternoon. All indications are that it was a complete success."

"But…?"

"I have to wear a weird-looking thing to bed. It's a very lame eye guard held on by tape. Not very dashing."

"Well, thank goodness I was never with you for your looks."

"Hey," he said, sounding wounded. But then he was kissing her again, and everything was perfect.

Especially the sound he made when he ran his hand up under her sundress.

"OKAY, WE'VE GOT EYES ON," Captain Miles said. The sensor operator at the simulator was completely focused on finding a particular white SUV in a huge parking lot that was filled with cars.

"Copy that." The drone pilot, Captain Zohan, seemed steady on the joystick, despite the fact that he and his teammate were the unlucky duo chosen to go through the challenge of not only finding that needle-in-a-haystack SUV, but doing it onstage in front of half their class in the big auditorium.

Sam was undergoing his own test, of a sort. His left eye wasn't at one hundred percent yet. It had only been three days since his surgery, and he was still sensitive to certain kinds of light, and had to keep up his regimen of eyedrops, but he'd told Colonel Stevens he was up to the task, and so far, so good.

"When it gets to a vehicle chase, I want a crew that's nonstop chatter," he said, after too long a silence. "For example, as a sensor operator I might notice there's a tiger-shaped infrared signature on the hood, so when it gets packed in a Baghdad traffic jam you'll be able to spot it."

The sensor operator's eyes narrowed and his shoulders visibly tensed.

"I'm not saying there is an IR signature on the SUV we're looking for. But there might be."

"I've got it," Miles said. "No, no, I've lost the target."

"So what do you do to get it back?"

"I'd zoom out and use my positive identification features."

Sam turned to his bigger audience. "Always work from big to small, big to small. We'll freeze the frame here for a moment, gentlemen."

The overhead projections of the simulator screens stopped at the same time as the simulators themselves. There was a certain light over the classroom that tended to halo at him, so he moved until the glare was gone. "Detail is everything in unmanned aviation. It's critical to hone your skills at the sweep and identify, even when you're not sitting in a sim. Try it at supermarkets, at concerts, at the park, in traffic.

"Your biggest opportunity for getting the skills you need is watching TV and movies. Look for inconsistencies and continuity mistakes. They're in practically everything we see, but they're usually small, like some man's sleeves rolled up in one angle, and the next angle of the same scene, the sleeves are down. It'll ruin your moviegoing experience, but it's a small price to pay when your attention to detail could mean the difference between life and death to one of our airmen."

"Sir." A lieutenant stood in the second row.

"Question?"

"With everything there on the screen, and with tracking down to the size of a pimple on some guy's ass, is this training going to be a hindrance to my efforts to move up to manned aircraft?"

Sam hadn't been expecting that. But he should have. There'd been one hell of a controversial article floating around about that very issue. "First of all, there is no up or down. RAVs are critical, perhaps the most critical weapon in our current arsenal. The data we track and survey is saving lives each and every day of this war. It's a new air force, a new kind of war, and we are on the cutting edge. The sooner we start looking at the bigger picture of where our duties lie, the better we all are. Without the man who tightens the screws, the machine is useless. We are airmen, and we are a singular force for freedom. Understood?"

"Yes, sir."

Sam scanned the crowd, not surprised to see Colonel Stevens standing in the back. Sam wondered if he'd passed his test, and if his answer to that young pilot was his own truth.

Turning back to the simulators, he returned to the tracking and marking of the SUV, more aware than he cared to be that he still couldn't quite get past the idea that piloting his F-16 wasn't better. There were few things on earth that compared to taking off in a fighter jet. But here, no one was at risk of equipment failure sending them spiraling to their deaths.

He knew, though, that given the choice Danny would never, not in a million years, choose to pilot an RPA instead of a jet. He wouldn't.

And now that Sam was facing the choice himself, he knew he wouldn't, either.

THE CLASSROOM EMPTIED quickly at lunch, but Sam made sure all the equipment was secured before leaving the stage area. He put a couple of drops in his left eye, then donned his sunglasses before he went out into the desert sun. Directly into the path of Colonel Stevens.

"Captain."

Sam saluted. "Sir."

"How are you doing?"

"We've got a lot of bright eager pilots. I think—"

"I meant your eyes."

"Fine, sir. The operation is looking like a success. I'm

scheduled to go back for a brief visit next week, but so far, all's well."

"You'll need to get checked out by our guys. I spoke to Dr. Emerson. He's very interested in your procedure. Frankly, I didn't follow the conversation after a certain point, but evidently, it could help a lot of airmen get qualified, even if they haven't gone through the initial surgery."

"That's my understanding, as well. I'll make sure to schedule an appointment with him, specifically."

"Good. And good job in there." The colonel nodded at the auditorium. "You're a hell of an instructor, Captain. We need more like you."

"Thank you, sir."

Stevens veered to the right toward his office, and Sam went left toward his, though he stopped halfway there. The sound of jets taking off behind him made him turn and look up to watch the elegance and beauty of those war birds as they punched into the sky.

There was nothing like it. Nothing.

15

SHARON'S HOUSE was in the Alamo Canyon area, not too far from where Emma lived, and she and Sam arrived with their cooler full of beer and burgers ten minutes late. It was sunset already, and only just after seven. She'd meant to come early to help set up, but somehow she'd gotten waylaid en route from the shower to the closet.

"We don't have to stay too late or anything," she said as she closed the trunk of the Mustang. Sam held the cooler as if it didn't have two cold twenty-packs inside, plus enough burgers to feed the block.

"Don't worry about me. I like barbecues, and it'll be fun meeting more of your gang."

"My gang. Yeah, we're a pretty rough bunch. We all carry red pens, and we're not afraid to use them."

They walked up the path to the stucco one-story house. Emma didn't bother to knock, which would have been useless anyway, as classic rock was blaring from the backyard.

As usual, the house was neat as a pin but with decor that could only have come from the crazy twosome who owned it. Never let it be said that Sharon and Joe Keeler ever let good taste get in the way of a good time.

Sam put the cooler down in the kitchen, but he had to

do a full three-sixty turn to appreciate the wonder of Sharon's interior design.

It began with cartoon cow salt-and-pepper shakers, and continued with cow hot pads, curtains, picture frames, figurines, plant holders and even a cow wall clock. "That's a lot of cows."

"Joe's just as bad, but he collects Western memorabilia. Wait till you see his office."

"Did they grow up on farms or something?"

"Sharon's from Chicago and Joe's from Cleveland. I doubt they've ever been on a ranch."

Sam nodded. "Joe does what at the base?"

"He's some sort of engineer."

Emma took Sam's hand, and they got a glimpse of the party through the sliding glass doors. The backyard had a big covered patio, and although it was tough to keep up in the summer, their lawn was actually green. Their hosts had festooned the fence and trees with sparkling white lights, the centerpiece of which was a big old hand-painted sign across the back bricks that said So Long, Summer, You Hot Bastard!

The very large gas barbecue was already smoking, and Emma's friends and their plus-ones were busy drinking and chattering away. There were very few active-service members in the group, considering. Although she knew of four spouses who worked as civilian employees at Holloman.

"There you are," Sharon said, and Emma grinned to see her oh-so-colorful friend done up as if she'd stepped out of a '50s film. Her dress was belted and big in the skirt, the better to show off her handmade country cow apron. Even her hair was pulled up in a ponytail. "Thought you two got lost."

She hugged Emma and then gave Sam the same treatment. "Glad you could make it, Captain. Come on back and have a beer. I'll start you off with some introductions, but after three, you're on your own."

"Sounds fair," he said, grabbing on to Emma's hand as he was led to a gathering of couples. Sam shook hands with Deanna and even remembered her name. She was with a tall guy Emma hadn't met before. Max had a shock of blond hair that was most definitely not a military cut, and she wished she could see better because it appeared he had a nose ring.

Then Sam was introduced to Perry, a history teacher who was very into the Civil War, and his wife, Haley, a stay-at-home mom of two. Emma looked around for Gary, but didn't see him, and she wondered if he'd decided to skip the party, which wasn't like him, or avoid Sam, which she hoped wasn't the case. He'd been great at school, never bringing up anything weird or making her uncomfortable.

Sam seemed completely at ease as he introduced himself to anyone he ran across. It looked as if he was already having a good time, but when he faced the tree draped with lights, he winced.

"Are you okay?" she asked, moving in close so only he could hear.

"Yeah, I'm fine. Why, do I seem nervous?"

"You're squinting. Are the lights bothering you?"

"It's nothing. Totally within normal parameters for a while. I get starbursts from a certain angle, but it doesn't hurt. I was thinking, though, of getting a drink. Can I get you something?"

"I'd love a beer."

"Really?"

"Yes," she said with a mock glare at his teasing. "It's a party. But I'm cutting myself off after one."

He gave her butt a light squeeze that no one could see,

then went off in search of the drinks. It was surprisingly hard to let him go. Not that he wouldn't be fine. He wasn't the life-of-the-party Danny'd been, but he was very good in social situations.

Everyone had liked Sam, back in the day, even though he'd sometimes get quiet. She used to wonder about that. He'd be going along fine, and then she'd notice him standing off to the side, watching. A sort of melancholy having set in for no obvious reason. But she'd never asked him about it. Frankly, Danny took up too much of her attention.

It didn't take Sam long to bring back not only the beer but also a trio of husbands that Emma knew, plus Max, and yes, that was a nose ring. One of the guys was asking about Sam's last tour in Afghanistan. Her chest tightened as if she hadn't already assumed his past would come up.

Being the new kid and the only fighter pilot in their circle, there were bound to be questions, and they wouldn't be about his work as an instructor. There was that damn mystique about fighter pilots. Soon, she knew, the women who'd met Sam five minutes ago would be looking at him differently. The blessing of the fighter jock and curse of the flyers' wives.

"So how come you're teaching and not flying?" Bill asked. He was married to Wendelin, who taught English to the German pilots who came to Holloman to train on the Raptors. "That has to suck."

"Are you kidding me?" Max said. "Dude, the drones are changing everything. They can get everywhere without being seen, and they're eyes in the sky 24/7. You do not want people operating those things who think they're playing some kind of video game."

Everyone looked at Max, probably as surprised as Emma was that he'd done so much thinking about drones.

He didn't look the type, but shame on her for judging him before they'd even spoken.

Sam nodded. "You couldn't be more right."

"My buddy from Berkeley is an RPA sensor out at Creech," Max said. "He tells me it's superstressful, and not just keeping alert for hours at a time, but to make damn sure you're making the right calls for the right reasons. No, seriously, hats off to you, man. Being a pilot's cool and all, but training hundreds of guys for that kind of responsibility? That's something. I mean, it's a big deal. The brass must have a lot of faith in you."

Emma found that her heart was beating faster by the second. As much as she wanted Sam's eyesight to be perfect, she hoped that by the time he was cleared for flight he'd be content with teaching. It was a foolish hope, she knew, but she couldn't help it.

She loved him, and she wanted him home. But staying out of the cockpit had to be Sam's choice. He'd be miserable, perhaps even resent her if he let her persuade him, which was why she would never even try. A motorcycle was one thing. Taking away his wings was something far more serious.

"No argument from me," Bill said. "Although you don't see a lot of teachers walking around in flight suits. I swear to God, those chick magnets must come with a written guarantee."

Sam smiled at the joke, but Emma would swear that he was thinking about Max's little speech. In fact, when Deanna pulled Max toward the grill, Sam stopped him. Shook his hand.

"Don't listen to him," Sharon said. "Sam doesn't need a flight suit to get the best woman in the world."

"That's probably true," Gary said, sneaking around the edge of the patio. "But it didn't hurt."

Emma stiffened, hoping he hadn't meant the remark in an unkind way, but she couldn't tell.

"Where've you been?" Sharon pulled Gary to the center of the crowd.

"Told you I was coming right back," he said. "And you can thank me later for filling the coolers with ice."

Emma took her beer from Sam, then captured his free hand in hers. "Sorry about that."

"About what? The questions? That's nothing."

"So, Sam," Bill said, moving in a little closer. "Seriously. Yeah, yeah, I get the whole teaching is noble thing, but what in hell made you trade in a cockpit for a classroom?"

Sam hesitated for a minute, then straightened his shoulders. "I had an issue with my vision about a year ago and was grounded. But I've had some corrective surgery that could help me qualify to fly again."

"Good for you, buddy," Bill said. "When will you hear?"

Emma looked from Bill to Sam, just in time to catch Sam's wink at her. "Don't know for sure. But it's looking good."

She sipped her beer and kept on smiling. Despite that little slice of wishful thinking, she'd already decided there was nothing to do about Sam's vision except take things one day at a time. She wouldn't be convinced that the repair was a success until he stopped getting starbursts and halos and could see without any problem or complications.

As for his going back to flying… She'd cross that bridge if and when. Nothing was going to be decided overnight. She knew that the military bureaucracy moved like glaciers. And she refused to get into a lather before things played out.

When she turned her head, she found Gary staring at her. He smiled, lifted his beer in a cheery salute. She couldn't imagine what he was thinking about this new twist, and she didn't care. She looked past him toward the house to see where Sharon had gone. He went back to listening to Bill and his friends talk about how they'd always wanted to know what it was like to be a Top Gun.

Sam didn't bother to tell them that was a navy thing, not air force. Why should he? The aura of speed and sex and high-flying danger was all anyone ever thought when they met a fighter pilot. The same things she'd tried to forget.

SAM HAD ALWAYS enjoyed grilling but something about turning a knob to settle the heat took some of the fun out of it. Still, even without coals, he knew his burgers. Medium rare had a certain feel, and he never got it wrong.

Most of the crowd had wanted ribs for dinner. He couldn't blame them, the one he'd tried had been delicious, but there were some die-hard burger fans. He wasn't sure if Emma had skipped the ribs out of loyalty or because she truly did like his burgers better. Either way, he was stupidly pleased. Especially when she moaned after taking her first bite.

They would not be staying late if he had anything to say about it.

"I guess you must hate Alamo," the woman waiting for her burger said. She was one of the only singles at the gathering. Mindy taught biology, and she might have had one beer too many. It had to be tough, though, coming to a party like this. Couples everywhere. Deanna's friend Max and Sam were the only two fresh faces.

He checked that the rare burger on the grill wasn't getting too warm, then smiled at Mindy before he looked at Emma, who was standing a little farther back. "Alamo has a lot going for it," he said. "For one thing, no humidity."

"Yeah, but it's dry as dirt here. In fact, if it wasn't for

the tons and tons of white sand, there wouldn't be anything but dirt in all of Southern New Mexico."

"I gather you're not fond of the desert?"

Mindy shook her head. "You have no idea."

"What keeps you here, then?"

"I like my job. The school's cool."

Emma joined them just as Sam put the buns on the grill. In another minute, he'd be finished at his station, most everyone having eaten their fill. Although he'd heard there was ice cream and pie for later.

Emma rubbed his back, and he caught the way Mindy pressed her lips together at the gesture. Sam was sure it wasn't anything personal. Although he was glad Emma was close.

"They're going to set up karaoke in about a half hour."

"That's a scary thought."

"Worse than dancing?" Emma asked with a grin.

"Neck and neck, I think. You don't want to hear me sing."

"I don't know. With your sexy baritone, I bet you sound great."

He gave Mindy her finished burger, and she just nodded before she left. As soon as she turned, he went back to Emma. "There's a reason you don't hear me singing in the shower."

"So what can you do, if you can't dance or sing?"

He put down his utensils, turned off the grill, then pulled Emma into his arms. His hand landed on her derriere, which he proceeded to squeeze. "I think we both know where my talents lie."

"I'll give it to you," she said, leaning in close so she could whisper in his ear. "You do make the best cup of coffee I've ever had."

He kissed her, and as his hand ran up her back, he

planned their exit strategy. Surely no one would miss them if they disappeared during karaoke.

"Hey, you two. Knock it off. This is a G-rated party."

Sam stepped away, holding his hands up. "I was minding my own business, Sharon. I swear."

"I'll bet. Emma, how about you come give me a hand with dessert, while He-man here helps Joe with…whatever."

Emma laughed. "When Sharon invites you to a barbecue, what she really wants is free labor," she said as Sharon tugged her in the direction of the house.

It turned out Emma was right. The *whatever* that Sharon had referred to was setting up a makeshift stage for the entertainment. Joe wasn't too thrilled about the task, either, but as he explained, there was a reason Sharon helped out with the drama department. She was a wannabe actress and singer who'd never had the chance to shine.

But there was a great deal of pride in his voice when he stopped unfurling the microphone cord to say, "You know, she's darn good, too. Better than half those folks on *American Idol* if you ask me."

The work itself wasn't difficult, and soon enough Sam was caught up in an all-guys' discussion about cars, his Mustang in particular. Seemed most of the men had either always wanted a muscle car, or had owned one in their earlier years.

Sam wondered why it was that even when the husbands and boyfriends congregated over typical guy talk, Gary was never around. When Sam had spoken to him, he'd been friendly enough. They'd never be best buddies, though. Besides, Gary didn't strike him as the kind of guy who'd own a souped-up classic Mustang.

By the time dessert was being served, all Sam could think about was being with Emma again. She'd been the best part of the evening, and while he didn't mind sharing her, he was looking forward to being home. In bed.

At least this wasn't like the old parties back when he, John and Danny were working for their wings. Those had had a lot more liquor, and a lot more testosterone floating around. For the first couple of years, Danny and Emma had been all over each other. But with time, Emma had ended up sitting with the air force groupies, or even left back at the house.

He wondered again if Emma knew that Danny hadn't always been faithful. *The damn fool.* He hadn't strayed often, at least as far as Sam knew, but even once was unacceptable.

Sam would cut off his own arm before he'd do that to her. When he got back to flying, it would be a whole new ball game. No hanging out at the officers' club, running off with the other pilots on adventure vacations. He would covet his time at home. With her. As often as the stereotype was flung around, he knew plenty of good family men who also happened to be fighter pilots. She'd never have to wonder where he was when he was at home base because he'd be with her.

"Sam," Joe said, "do me a favor and go give the gals a hand with the desserts, huh? I want to make sure the music is all set."

"Sure thing." Sam headed toward the kitchen, listening to odd bits of conversation peppered with the loud squeal of the microphone feedback.

He'd just entered the house when he stopped at the sound of his name. Gary was the one saying it, and he must have been just around the corner.

"…he'll be flying again. He has to be pretty thrilled about that. Though I can't imagine you are."

Sam had thought he heard Emma's voice, and assumed

that was who Gary was talking to, but what a messed-up thing for him to say. Nobody answered.

"Of course I am," Emma finally said. "I want Sam to be happy. Anyway there's no guarantee he will be flying. He has to put in a request to transfer. Even if he does that, it doesn't necessarily mean he's going to get a plane."

Emma sounded defensive, but she hadn't asked what Gary meant by that last remark. What bothered Sam even more had been her delayed response. What the hell was that about? Did Gary know something Sam didn't?

"Well, I hope it all works out for you," Gary said. "Honestly, I do, Emma. You deserve to be happy, too."

There was another stretch of silence. Maybe Emma had paused to take a drink or do something that Sam had mistaken for hesitation. No need to be paranoid. He was about to step into the kitchen, when Emma said, "I believe you do wish the best for me. I appreciate it."

"That's because it's true." Gary's voice had lowered. "Just remember, I'll be here for you if you ever need me."

Behind Sam, there were footsteps, and he moved aside as a couple whose names escaped him went around the wall. Now Gary was just being a dick. Maybe that was what that silence had been about earlier. She probably figured it was better to ignore him. As much as Sam wished he could turn around instead of pretending he didn't want to kick Gary's ass, he had no choice but to go inside and get the damn ice cream.

THE FIRST THING Emma wondered when she saw Sam enter the kitchen was if he'd overheard her conversation. Gary hadn't said anything damning. Well, yeah, he had, that one remark, but that was a couple minutes ago so Sam couldn't have heard. But she still felt uncomfortable. So she'd been a dope swearing off pilots in front of her friends—she still wasn't about to discuss Sam with Gary.

The thing was, she did believe him. She thought he wanted the best for her. Now, maybe he worried that with Sam getting back his wings, he wasn't the right man for the life Emma wanted. But it wasn't Gary's business, even if he meant well.

Still, she couldn't blame him for thinking that. Which was, she realized, why her stomach was tensing with guilt. She wasn't sure, either.

Things had changed so much in such a short period of time. If felt as if they'd been on an island of happiness for a couple of weeks, and then everything had started spiraling out of control. Sam was so excited about the possibility of flying again that she hadn't dared share her misgivings. Nor had she admitted how terrified she'd been when he'd flown back from L.A. But even though she'd tried her best to stay in the moment, to not think the worst, she had.

She supposed that was the thing about experiencing true tragedy. Before Danny had been killed, she'd thought he was invincible. He behaved as if nothing could touch him. They all had, those young warriors. They owned the world from thirty thousand feet.

Then the illusions had been shattered, and she couldn't ever believe the illusions again. Bad things happened. Really bad things. God, she didn't know if she could handle it, the waiting, the constant panic building inside with irrational certainty that, like Danny, someday Sam wouldn't make it home.

"I was told I could find something sweet in here," Sam said. He nodded at Gary as he passed him, and put his arm around Emma's shoulder. "It's true. You look good enough to eat."

"I'm sure everyone would prefer pie and ice cream, and

there's a bunch to take out," Emma said. "What are you better at, balancing or withstanding the cold?"

"Normally, balancing, but I'd better carry the ice cream."

She carefully avoided looking at Gary and kissed Sam's cheek, because that had to be hard to admit while he was in the middle of showing off his peacock feathers. "Just so you know, you're wonderful."

His smile made things better. Not perfect. But better. She pointed to the subzero stand-alone freezer. "Could you take one of the big tubs out to the table?"

He opened the freezer door. "Just how much ice cream are we supposed to eat tonight?"

Emma laughed, so did Gary. They both sounded forced. "She's hosting an ice-cream social for the drama club and their sponsors next week. Another fund-raiser."

"Ah. Okay. I'll be back in a minute to grab whatever else I can."

Between the three of them, they got all four pies, the ice cream, toppings and all the necessary flatware out to the tables just as the first song started on the main stage.

Sam took a decent slice of cherry pie with a vanilla scoop, and Emma went for the apple à la mode she no longer wanted. But she'd mentioned wanting dessert several times, and if she skipped it Sam would know something was wrong.

He found them a nice patch of grass to sit on. They had a fence to lean against, and they were out of Joe's line of sight as he cajoled people up to sing.

After they'd finished eating, Sam pulled her around until she was leaning against his chest, his arms around her middle. She loved resting against him, reveling in the strength of him, and their closeness. But she couldn't deny that her thoughts about their future weren't nearly as rosy as they'd been.

She wanted him whole and safe and home. And she wanted him happy. There was so much she wanted to do with Sam. Marriage, kids, all of it. The whole foolish dream, complete with a swing set in the backyard and soccer games and anniversary parties and growing old together.

But she'd seen his whole countenance change when he talked about being a pilot. She heard the thrill in his voice even when he was trying not to get overexcited. She understood that, she did. Danny had been like that. John, too. And although Sam might have the best of intentions, he was the man Gary had warned her about.

The question was, could Sam put her first, even when he was an active duty fighter pilot? And would she be able to stand it if he couldn't?

She would have to. Because she'd reached the point of no return.

He kissed her temple. "You okay?"

"I'm…good," she said, listening to Sharon belt out a song from *Les Miz.* "Glad that you're with me."

"Me, too, honey," he said, squeezing her tight.

She squeezed him right back, wishing she was strong enough to hold him like this and never let him go.

16

"SORRY I'M SO BREATHLESS," Sam said, adjusting his seat belt one-handed while he held his cell in the other. "I made this flight by the skin of my teeth. The gate was practically in another state, so I had to run the whole way. Am I interrupting?"

"Are you kidding?" Emma said, her voice a balm that never failed to soothe. "Tell me what they said. Are you okay? Will you have to go back?"

He smiled. Despite the fact that he'd assured her everything was fine and that he was in no danger, he got that her concern was genuine. "I'm better than fine. The surgeon and the ophthalmologist were really pleased. They ran every test. I can't imagine I won't pass the base check. I'll still need to wear a contact in the one eye, but it's a minor correction. I'm like 20/30 without, so it looks like a go on all engines."

"Wow," she said, but her voice was low. Hushed. "That's good. That's great. So, you go to the eye doctor here, and then you put in for a transfer to a cockpit job, right?"

"Yep. Of course nothing will happen this training cycle, and the way things move, it'll probably be longer than that, but I know Colonel Stevens is going to push for me, so—"

"I thought he wanted you to stay as an instructor."

"Yeah, he'd like me to, but I think he understands that I want to get a jet. Maybe we'll work a deal that when this tour is up, I'll come back to the RPA program."

"You've talked about that?"

"Not yet. Not in so many words, and I won't until I have the clearance to fly. I didn't want to jump the gun."

"Sure," she said, but she sounded off.

He'd figured his clean bill of health would have made her happy. "Is everything okay?"

She didn't answer for a minute, and he strained, listening for background noise, but sitting on a runway waiting for takeoff wasn't exactly quiet. "You know what? My next meeting's gonna start in a minute."

"Right, this was your department review, right?"

"Yep, and after that is the all-faculty meeting, so I'm probably going to be stuck here until after you get home. It'll be dark when you land. Will you be able to drive okay?"

"Oh, yeah. My eyes aren't even dilated."

"All right. You have to promise to call me as soon as you land. Leave a message if I can't pick up."

"I will. After you're free maybe we could meet for dinner? I'll take you someplace fancy to celebrate."

"I'm sorry, I've got to go. Promise you won't forget to call."

"Promise,"

"Good. Be safe."

"Emma?" he said, but she'd already gone. Had he heard a tremble in her voice? What the hell? Was she still worried after all his assurances? No, she knew his eye was fine.

Ever since the party, things between them had been... Not bad. Just different. It wasn't as if he expected her to be happy all the time, but he'd caught her looking at him, like this morning when he'd been rushing to get to the base for his plane. She'd seemed sad, worried. And he had been in such a rush, he hadn't asked her. Maybe there was something at her work that wasn't going well. Like Gary giving her more crap. She hadn't mentioned her conversation with him at the party, and Sam hadn't asked about that, either. He didn't expect her to tell him every little thing in her life. She had a right to privacy.

But that didn't alter the fact that he'd been so caught up in getting his vision repaired he'd been a pretty lousy boyfriend.

That sounded weird. Boyfriend wasn't even close to the relationship he and Emma had. Significant other made him want to hit something, and partner was just as awful. It was probably too soon, but he wanted to move to the next step, although he wasn't a hundred percent sure if that was what Emma wanted.

His thoughts lost out to the ruckus happening across the row in front of Sam.

The flight attendant was trying to calm down an older lady who was on her cell. They couldn't take off or even lock down the plane until the woman turned off her phone. It was instantly obvious that the woman was panicking. Even from Sam's seat, he could see her shaking.

"Please, if I can just talk to my husband during take-off, I'll be fine."

"I'm so sorry, ma'am, but we can't allow a telephone to be live on takeoff. It can interfere with the electronics of the plane."

"Oh, God. Tom, they won't let me talk to you."

"You'll have to turn off the cell now, ma'am. I'm sorry, but we're holding up other flights. Do you understand?"

The woman nodded, but still didn't obey. "I love you,"

she said, turning her head away from the attendant. "I love you and the kids. Don't ever doubt that. If I don't see you again, I've left everything in the wall safe. Except for the banking details, and those are in the desk."

"Ma'am, you're going to be fine. It's more dangerous getting to the airport than it is to fly. I have to insist you turn off the phone now, or I'll be forced to get security involved."

Sam shook his head, sorry for the crew member but sorrier for the woman. He understood that fear of flying was a common phobia. It was so far off his radar that he had a tendency to dismiss it as foolish. But the woman couldn't help it. She was still visibly shaking. The young lady sitting next to her was trying to offer comfort, but it didn't appear to be working.

Maybe the frightened woman had lost someone in a crash. That would explain a— He stopped. Breathing, moving. How had he not seen it? God, he was an idiot. Emma had lost Danny in a freak accident. She wasn't just worried about Sam's eye; she was worried he wouldn't make it home. Like Danny hadn't.

She'd probably gotten up that morning thinking everything was fine. Maybe she'd spoken to Danny before work, made plans for his car to be transported to Alamo, or talked about the weather, or just nothing. It was a day like any other. Until someone from the chaplain's office had shown up at her door.

Jesus.

Was that what Gary had meant at the party about Emma not being thrilled Sam could get his wings back? Did Gary know her better than Sam?

He'd planned on doing some reading on the flight back, but he left his book in his stowed bag. He needed to show her the test results. Nothing he could say would ease Emma's mind, not without proof. He'd figured that would take care of everything once and for all. But shit, had he missed the mark.

He remembered hearing about Danny's accident. The first thing Sam did after gaining his senses was to call Emma. She'd been in shock. He'd told her he'd take leave, that he could be with her in a couple of hours, and she'd turned him down flat.

How many times had he wanted to call her during that first year? But after the funeral, she'd made it really clear that seeing him and John was too difficult. It hadn't mattered that they'd only wanted to comfort her, to share in that grieving and whatever healing was possible. She'd said she needed space, and he'd honored her wishes.

It had been terrible. The hardest year he'd ever had. He'd never lost anyone before, not anyone close. His grandfather had died, but Sam hadn't known him well. His grandmother had died before he'd been born. It had always been his mom and him. Then he'd met John and Danny, and he'd had brothers.

Emma wasn't particularly close to her family. There was a sister, but they only seemed to speak or see each other on occasions, and she had only mentioned her folks once or twice, but with no real affection.

It didn't matter that she and Danny had been headed for a breakup. Sam knew for sure that they loved each other. Not being able to make it wasn't the same as falling out of love. Danny hadn't been careful enough with Emma. He'd taken her for granted, and now, so had Sam.

He should have taken more care. Made sure to check in with her every step of the way, even if it was just voice mails or texts while she was in class. He would call the minute they parked at the gate. Let her know she could breathe again. Then he'd take her out and make sure she knew how amazing she was. Show her that he was someone she could count on.

EMMA PARKED HER CAR on the street, even though Sam had told her to use his garage. She'd never taken him up on it because her car was functional, bought for practicality, and if something happened to it she would be more inconvenienced than upset.

The Mustang, however, was a prized possession, a machine that was loved and cared for. That represented the part of Sam that loved danger and speed and excitement. Emma needed the reminder.

She got the champagne out of the car, thankful the base kept good bubbly in the refrigerator case all the time. Tonight she and Sam were going to celebrate. Well, Sam would celebrate, and she would do her best to be happy for him.

He'd been a sweetie when he'd called to let her know he was disembarking and that it would still be a while until he made it home. She'd relaxed immediately...up to a point.

The faculty meeting had been the shortest one she could ever remember. She'd sat between Gary and Sharon, and they must have picked up on her mood because they hadn't done their usual kidding around. In fact, she'd clearly had her shields up because the three of them had barely talked.

Emma was almost sorry she hadn't confided in Sharon. Gary, though... What he'd said at the party had been on her mind ever since. Resenting him wasn't fair. He wasn't to blame for the situation. No one was. She hadn't expected Sam. And she certainly hadn't planned on falling in love with him. Would she be in this situation if he'd come to Holloman as a pilot? She didn't think so.

Although it embarrassed her to admit it, she'd hoped

that Sam wouldn't qualify to fly. Yes, she loved him. Very much. But was love going to be enough?

It wasn't that she assumed he would be like Danny—leaving her so he could go off and party with his friends. Although she couldn't prove it, she was reasonably certain Danny had cheated on her. But that wasn't the part she was worried about with Sam.

The car. The bike. His determination to be in a cockpit again. All of those things were part of his makeup. There was a reason he'd hung out with John and Danny, and not just because they'd been roommates at the Air Force Academy. They were like brothers, and they lived for the rush, and that was at the heart of her dilemma.

Could she bear worrying every time he climbed into the cockpit?

On the other hand, could she bear to let Sam go?

He'd made her so happy these past weeks. Happier than she'd ever imagined she could be. There was so much to love about Sam. He was solid. A man who might leave the screwdriver out, but he took his job seriously, was thoughtful of her on a daily basis. He'd gone out of his way to be there when she needed him. Even more spectacularly, when she'd wanted him.

Just the week before last, she'd gone to help Sharon paint scenery at the auditorium. Sam had offered to come, but then he'd gotten a call to join a group of active fighter pilots for a round of golf. It was an important invitation. Sam had bonded with his fellow pilots everywhere he'd been stationed, but things were different as a teacher. The golf game had been his ticket to the inner circle, and he'd declined.

At first she'd thought it was because he hadn't wanted to be associated with the Reaper pilots, but he'd come right out and told her he'd rather spend the day hanging out with her.

She put the champagne in the fridge then made a reservation for two at Stella Vita.

When she hung up, all she could think was that life wasn't fair. That wasn't news, of course, and it was a childish thought, but come on, what kind of a cruel trick was it to send this incredible man into her life in the most perfect situation imaginable, only to pull the rug out from under her after she'd lost her heart?

Why couldn't this surgery have come later, after he'd taught for a couple of years? Sam would have missed the cockpit, yes, but once he'd seen the spread of effects from his teaching, he wouldn't be able to deny the importance of his influence. She'd been thrilled with Max's little speech at the barbecue, and she'd hoped it had started Sam thinking about his invaluable contribution.

Unless he could arrive at the conclusion on his own, there was no way she could convince him that being an instructor was more important than flying. He'd wanted to be a fighter pilot since he was a kid. That didn't just vanish because he had other talents.

So he would be a flyer again. Which meant transfers every few years. He'd be sent into combat situations and she'd be left behind. Waiting. Panicking. Shattering piece by piece under the weight of fear that the chaplain would show up at her door again. She wasn't sure she had it in her.

When she finally heard the garage door open, she focused on the moment, on the fact that he was healthy and whole and that this was a triumphant moment for him. He had no idea, she was certain, what the prospect of his taking to the air again was doing to her. And she wasn't going to tell him. Not tonight. Tonight was for champagne.

She met him at the door and just like the first time she'd

seen him at Stella Vita, her body reacted—a wonderful electric shock, if there could be such a thing. For a moment she just stared at him, forgetting to breathe, thinking of nothing except *he's here, thank God*. She was drawn to him with the power of the tides, and as soon as she was in his arms nothing else mattered.

He smiled into her hair, surrounded her with his scent and a quiet hum of pleasure. Time seemed to stretch and the rest of the world backed off.

Two minutes later, maybe three, he pulled back, looked at her, kissed her. Not the hungry kind, the prelude to getting naked as quickly as possible, but a slow melting together. As tenderly as if she might break.

"I'm so glad you're here," she said when they parted.

"Me, too. You're all I thought about on the way home. I'd have hitchhiked if I'd had to."

"I'm glad it wasn't necessary. But you must be tired. All that travel in one day."

"I'm fine now." He squeezed her shoulders before he let her go and picked up the satchel he'd brought with him. "I've got all the papers in here. The notes from the doctors, everything. Both of my eyes are healthy and there's no reason to think there will be any complications."

"Thanks," she said. "I believe you."

"Still." He pulled out a file folder, and she took it. Most of the papers meant nothing to her. Numbers that had no context. But she'd skim the notes later.

"So there's nothing standing in your way now," she said. "You can go back to flying anytime."

"I may have, in my enthusiasm, slightly exaggerated the ease with which I'd get back in the cockpit. The eye doctors here have to give me their blessings, and that's not a lock no matter what the surgeons say. My peripheral vision is critical, and there are tests they perform that the surgeons don't."

"But you were so sure you'd pass." She had to stay calm. Not sound hopeful at his expense.

"Anticipation will do that to a guy. But now that the whirlwind is over, I'll still have to put in a request to transfer, and there has to be an opening for me to fill, which may not happen for a while. You know the drill."

The way Sam studied her, and his new banked enthusiasm, it all confused her. "Is there something else wrong?"

"No. No, I just don't want us to put all our eggs in that one basket. I may be able to fly again, but then again, I'll pretty much go where the brass tells me to go. For now, that's the classroom."

He was right. In fact, he was saying the same things she'd been trying to believe. That the future wasn't written, that anything could happen.

But that anything included him in a cockpit. Her worrying every day whether he was going to come home or not. Equally troubling was how he would change once he was living a fighter pilot's life. The camaraderie, the contagion of the need for thrills that she'd seen take on more and more of Danny's attention.

It was important to remember Sam wasn't her late husband, but perhaps more important for her to be realistic.

"What's that frown about?" he asked.

"Frown? I wasn't... I got champagne." She turned to the kitchen. "And I made reservations for dinner."

He captured her arm before she took a second step. "Champagne?"

She nodded, her smile genuine. "You're better. You don't have to worry about not seeing well enough anymore. That's cause for celebration, don't you think?"

"You're amazing, you know that?"

She shrugged. "I'm so happy for you."

His smile seemed confusingly sad, or perhaps more bittersweet. "Are you really hungry?"

She shook her head.

"Come to bed with me?" He bracketed her face with gentle hands as he stared into her gaze. "I want you so much."

"Me, too."

"I want to make love with you. Now."

She was still a bit shaky, but there was no way to turn that invitation down. Of course she'd make love with him. Every chance she could get, even though it wouldn't make her decision any easier. There was simply no getting over the fact that she loved him. It might kill her in the end, but for today, she was his.

Once they were in the bedroom, Sam took her clothes off with care. He was in no rush, and while she probably should have called Stella Vita, she wouldn't interrupt him for the world.

As her blouse parted, he kissed her chest, just under her collarbone. Slipping off her bra brought more kisses, gentle breaths and sweet lips that gave her goose bumps and made her sigh.

She ran her hands through his hair, trailed her fingers across his temples and cheeks as he unbuttoned and kissed his way down her body until she was naked. He hadn't removed any part of his uniform, and it was deeply erotic to be bared as he rose slowly, letting his hands glide across her flesh.

"You're the most beautiful woman I've ever seen," he said, his voice hushed as if he'd told her a secret.

It would have been easy to roll her eyes at the hyperbole, but when she met his gaze it was clear he was telling her the truth. Of course he was. He might not have said those exact words before, but he'd shown her. With touches and kisses and smiles and looks, and she never felt anything less than beautiful when she was with him.

It was time for him to lose his clothes, because all she wanted was to be in his arms, to snuggle close, to find that perfect peace that came in the aftermath.

The thought of leaving him was as unwelcome as a splash of ice water, and she refused to entertain it for more than a second.

She didn't have to make up her mind right now. Not even later tonight or tomorrow, and probably not the next day. She could wait and see how things would roll out. With each passing hour anything could happen. He could change his mind about flying, or not get the clearance, or find that being an instructor was more to his liking. A hundred things she had no control over, except the decision to cut herself off from the opportunity to watch it unfold.

It was also possible that she could come to terms with his choice to go back to flying.

Fumbling with his pants, he took over the job of undressing with great speed and skill. It only took them a moment to climb under the sheets, to press against each other.

He kissed her and she kissed him back. His hum returned as they took their time, and she touched him in all the places that he particularly liked.

She knew him so well, and he had memorized her in return. When he ran his flattened tongue on her neck and let it rest against her pulse point, she reached for his wrist and felt his heartbeat at the same time.

His was strong and quick and hers sped up as he slipped his knee between her thighs and pressed up tight.

When her head fell back at the pressure *right there,* he moved until his warm breath washed over the shell of her ear. "I can't believe I found you again," he whispered.

"I'm such a lucky bastard. If it were mine, I'd give you the world."

She let go of his wrist and touched his face again. "I don't want the world," she said. "Just you."

THE SOUND of the garage door closing was enough to get Emma's heart beating double time. She'd been trying to decide if they should have the discussion over dinner or after, and she'd chosen to have a pleasant meal, even if she wasn't sure she'd be able to eat.

With that in mind, she'd made a casserole when she got home from work. Cooking had given her something to do with her hands, although it hadn't distracted her. She was still a mess thinking about what she had to do. Tonight she would tell Sam the truth about her reaction to his becoming a flyer. That it scared her, and that it was probably going to take counseling to address her fears. But that she was also willing to do whatever it took to be with him.

Maybe wine would've been better than the ginger ale she'd switched to in the hope of settling her stomach.

She heard the doorknob and braced herself for a difficult evening, one in which she wouldn't lose her courage just because Sam was in the room.

He smiled the instant he saw her, looking happier than he had all week…as if he'd just opened the best Christmas gift ever. She smiled back, reminding herself this was what she wanted, for Sam to be happy, but that didn't mean it wouldn't come at a cost.

"Hey, beautiful," he said, walking toward her, keeping one hand behind his back so she couldn't see what he was holding.

"Hey, yourself." This wasn't just about the eye exam this morning. They'd spoken briefly, so she knew that had gone well. Something else had lit a fire in his eyes.

Sadly, she knew what it had to be. Nothing short of an imminent transfer back to a cockpit would make Sam Brody this happy. He couldn't live without flying, and seeing him now, she wouldn't have asked him to.

He stopped just in front of her, leaned in for a quick kiss, then held out a springtime bouquet. Carnations, pink roses, daisies and lilies.

She blinked at his offering. "What's this for?"

"Can't a man bring his girlfriend flowers?"

"You haven't before."

"I know. I realized that at the shop. I didn't even know what kind you like or what to get. But I should... I absolutely should know something like that. It's important."

"They're lovely. They really are, and you chose perfectly. But you don't have to bring me flowers. Or anything special. Just you. That's all I need."

His smile wavered, then vanished altogether. "There's something else I realized today. I could've kicked myself when I finally got what was going on." He brushed the side of her cheek with gentle fingers, and she leaned into the touch even though she was completely confused.

"What on earth are you talking about?" She clutched the front of his shirt, then willed herself to relax. "Is this about your flight status? Did you get transferred already?"

Sam's brow wrinkled in confusion. "What? No." He shook his head. "I haven't even submitted the paperwork."

"But I saw a copy on your desk."

"That's the original," he said. He looked somber. "Let's sit, okay?"

She nodded, and he led her to the couch. They both sat, their thighs touching, his hand wrapped around hers.

"From the beginning all you wanted was to be friends. I pushed, I— Hell, I'd called you as soon as I got to town. I wasn't sure if it would be uncomfortable for you. I didn't want to open old wounds, but even when I tried talking myself out of making the call I couldn't. As soon as I heard they were sending me here all I could think about was seeing you again."

What was this about? Regret? Did he think contacting her had been a mistake? Was he about to deliver the whole it's me, not you spiel? No, that wasn't like Sam. She had to quiet her thoughts. Just listen. It wasn't easy. "I'm so glad you made that call."

"Me, too. But despite my best intentions, I've managed to do exactly that. Open old wounds."

"What?"

"This whole business with the surgery has been pretty uncomfortable for you."

"I—" She stopped her argument before it got started when Sam held up his hand.

"It took me a while to realize just how uncomfortable. That first trip—I was hopping planes without a second thought, and then when I let my cell battery run out… Not hearing from me had to be difficult. It must have brought back awful memories."

She needed to tell him he was right even though her throat was tight and she wasn't sure she could speak, but from the way he nodded, her expression had clearly given it away. Okay, this was a good thing, his understanding what she'd been going through. It opened the door for more conversation. Difficult conversation, but critical.

After a hard swallow and a nod, she said, "If it's any consolation, I didn't know that would happen until you'd left that first time. I started flashing back to the day I was told about Danny. It wasn't crippling, so I'm hoping that in time, I'll get better. I can always go back for more counseling."

"Wait a minute. First, it's not your fault, and it's not

something you should have to deal with. It was a natural reaction and I should've seen it coming."

"No."

"Yes." He shook his head, self-recrimination written all over his face. "My ego has been invested in me being a fighter pilot for a very long time. It was hard to look past that. I got it in my head that you deserved that same hotshot I used to be. It's not an excuse, but it's the truth."

"Oh, sweetie, what I feel for you has nothing to do with your flight status."

His eyes narrowed as he held her gaze. "That's it. That's how I feel about you."

"I don't understand."

He looked so serious. "The way I feel about you is that the right thing is for me to be here for you. To do my damnedest to make sure you feel safe and cared for. I don't ever want you to worry about me. And to bring home your favorite flowers just because," he said, giving in to a smile that only lasted until she shook her head.

"I can't ask you to give up flying. I love you, and I want you to be happy."

He inhaled deeply. "You love me," he said, as if he could hardly believe it.

She nodded. It was far too late to deny it. Not that she would. "I do. Very, very much."

Sam leaned over and kissed her. It was a little too hard and not at all smooth, but it left no doubt that he had no objections to the sentiment. Pulling back, his smile made him look like the kid he'd been back in his academy days. "Is it any wonder I want to give you the world? Honey, you don't have to ask me to give up flying. I want to."

She stared at him for a long moment, trying to understand what he was saying. The offer he'd just made. It was tempting to jump all over it, make him swear, put it in writing. But she couldn't stop being honest now. Not when so much was at stake. "Was that part of your revelation today?"

"Part of it, yeah."

She slipped her hands from his, and curled them tightly in her own lap. "That's not a spur-of-the-moment kind of decision. It's wonderful, and I appreciate it, but you yourself said you've been invested in being a pilot your whole life. Not an instructor. That's huge, and the last thing on earth I want is for you to regret it."

He nodded, meeting her gaze, not flinching, not even blinking. "The day before I went for my follow-up exam, I knew my vision was good. I knew in my gut I'd qualify again. I was so sure that I filled out the transfer papers the night before I left so I could turn them in the day after I returned. But there was this woman, another passenger, on the commercial flight I took. She was hysterical, convinced she wouldn't make it home to her family.

"I felt bad for her at first, but I let it roll off. Fear of flying is so alien to me. But I'd never seen anyone freak out like that. And then it hit me. I'd made you relive that horrible day you were told Danny was gone. It made me sick that I'd been so oblivious. That started the ball rolling."

"Oh, Sam." She looked into his earnest green eyes. "Wanting to do the nice thing isn't necessarily the right thing."

His head tilted to the right as he leaned a few inches closer. "Do you have any idea how long I've loved you?"

She sucked in a breath and held it. Even after he'd shown her that he felt the same way she did, to hear the words was amazing.

"Jesus, Emma, you were my best friend's wife, and I still couldn't stop myself from wanting you. When you told me you were going to ask Danny for a divorce, I almost felt relieved, as if that somehow absolved me." He scrubbed at his face. "How messed up is that?"

"Stop that. Now. Neither one of us is perfect, and I had some of my own feelings that I wouldn't have wanted Danny to know. But we both loved him."

"In our own way."

Emma had to grin. "You're such a *guy*."

"That's true. But my story's not over, so..."

She nodded, her gaze stuck on his, needing to watch him as well as hear every word.

"I was in the classroom this afternoon. Forty-two students were at their computers, and we were running through some maneuvers. This one guy, he goes to make a loop. You can't make a loop with a Reaper, that's not what they're designed for. It was kind of a joke, you know, because in this well-known flight simulator video game that's how you get out of a complicated situation, so there was a lot of laughter, and I put a stop to it, right then. There's no room for that kind of thing, not on duty, and when you're in the classroom, you're on duty, and I don't care that it's not a real Reaper, you do not go off script, not for anything."

"Okay," she said, not at all sure where this was going.

"I dressed him down, but I used the opportunity to talk about the rush a pilot feels when he's in the air, and how that's not something he can count on with an RPA. That if that's what he's looking for in this gig, he should think twice. Become a cop or a paramedic or a race car driver. And then it hit me. I don't need to get my kicks by flying jets. Not even a Raptor. Not even a damn rocket to the moon."

He captured her right hand and held it just shy of too tightly. "I'm not that guy anymore. You know where I feel that rush? When I turn on our street. Doesn't matter if we're staying here or at the other house, I turn on that street and I can feel my heart start to race. I actually need to use cruise control so that I don't speed. And when I finally see you? It takes a long time for me to settle back down, and sometimes that doesn't happen until after we've made love."

"Really?" She wanted so badly to believe him. And she did, but what if he'd been carried away by the moment? How could he compare seeing her with the exhilaration of flying Mach 2?

"Really. Honey, I'm so sorry for putting you through one second of fear. I wish I could take that away. But I'm not sorry I had the surgery. Knowing I can fly made it much clearer that I don't need to."

Her whole body changed, hearing, believing, what he'd just said. It was as if she'd been wearing a corset for ages and finally the cursed thing was off and she could breathe again. "Wow," she said. "You do mean it."

"I love you, Emma. I am crazy in love with you. I hope this doesn't come as too much too soon, but I want us to be together forever. I want us to have kids, and to watch them grow up. I want to be with you when we're old, and I don't want to do it by sharing more than half my time with the air force.

"I want to keep on being an instructor. Go to work in the morning, come home in time for dinner, at least mostly. I want to be your husband first, and an officer second."

That breath Emma had just regained had been stolen right back. Because this was too much, too close to her fantasies to be real.

His demeanor changed with a softening of his gaze and the lowering of his shoulders. He leaned toward her so that she could see his laugh lines and how unfairly long his eyelashes were. As if he meant to kiss her, but he stopped short. "Oh, sweetheart, all I've done is take away my blinders. The reason it all came together like this was because the truth had been there for weeks, if not longer. I choose you, and I hope like hell you choose me."

She felt the heat of tears come to her eyes, and she didn't want to cry. It was so girlie and so cliché, but her body had a will of its own, and the tears came. No sobbing, thank goodness, but blinking wasn't enough to stop the slow and steady drops. "I love you back, you insane man. I want all those things, too."

"You're sure now?" he asked. "I don't want you to have any misgivings."

Putting her hand on his cheek she said, "Not a one."

He closed the gap between them with a kiss that brought fresh tears even as it curled her toes. A future with Sam at her side was the best thing she could imagine.

Six months later...

SAM LOOKED INCREDIBLY handsome in his service dress uniform. With his broad shoulders and long legs, he could be on a recruiting poster, but Emma was glad he wasn't. She wanted him all to herself.

But for now, she could share him. After all, he was the best man at a very important wedding. John Devlin and Cassie O'Brien were tying the knot, and every time Emma looked at the happy couple on the makeshift platform that had been built for the ceremony, she teared up. She was so happy for her old friend, so glad to have John back in her life, and it didn't hurt that she really liked Cassie.

The first time Emma had been to Cassie's brother's bar had been two days ago. She'd never have believed so much could be accomplished to transform the not-quite-dive joint into something so festive. The colors were blue and white, of course, and there were garlands and blue hydrangeas on the tables set up in the back. The wedding cake topper was a handcrafted showstopper—the groom was a captain in uniform, the bride a very good likeness of Cassie, with her curly auburn hair and beautiful smile, in a replica of her knee-length white dress, right down to the tulle crisscross neckline.

Cassie's friend Lisa stood as her maid of honor, and the lovely girl hadn't stopped crying through the whole ceremony.

But now they were down to the final moments, the exchange of vows and the rings. The tears Emma had managed to blink back fell down her cheeks, and thank goodness she'd remembered to bring tissues. Not that she cared about her makeup. This was a moment of pure joy and perhaps a preview of what was to come for her and Sam.

By the time the new bride and groom kissed, the whole eclectic assembly were on their feet, applauding and whooping it up. Not just the Gold Strike bar's regulars, but all the uniformed airmen were letting loose, loudly. And they hadn't even opened the champagne yet.

The happy couple walked down the aisle, followed by Sam and Lisa. Sam met Emma's gaze as he passed, and his eyes were suspiciously shiny.

When he came back from his official duties, Sam pulled her into his arms and kissed her as though they were alone in their home back in Alamo. She thought about all that had happened since that first dinner. How he'd become such a highly regarded instructor, how wonderful it was to have him come home to her every night, to wake up to him every morning. How she was happier than she would have ever imagined.

"So, I'm thinking," Sam said, after taking a much needed breath, "that this wedding thing has some merit."

"Really?" The passion and love in his gaze made her melt.

He nodded. "Today is for John and Cassie," he said, running a gentle finger along her cheekbone. "But do me a favor. When it comes time for her to toss that bouquet?"

Emma held her breath as her smile widened. "Yes?"

"Catch it."

* * * * *

COMING NEXT MONTH FROM

HARLEQUIN *Blaze*

Available August 20, 2013

#763 THE CLOSER • *Men Out of Uniform*
by Rhonda Nelson

Former ranger Griff Wicklow mastered the art of removing a woman's bra in high school, but protecting one worth two million dollars is another matter altogether. Especially when the real gem is the jeweler along for the ride....

#764 MISSION: SEDUCTION • *Uniformly Hot!*
by Candace Havens

Battle-scarred marine Rafe McCawley is in need of relaxation, but when he meets gorgeous pro surfer Kelly Callahan in Fiji, resting is the last thing on his mind!

#765 MYSTERY DATE
by Crystal Green

A woman craving sensual adventure. A lover who hides his identity in the shadows. An erotic interlude that takes each of them farther than they've ever dared to go....

#766 THE DEVIL SHE KNOWS
by Kira Sinclair

One incredible night with a mysterious bad boy in a red silk mask—that's all Willow Portis wants. Too bad she doesn't recognize her devil until it's too late....

REQUEST YOUR FREE BOOKS!
2 FREE NOVELS PLUS 2 FREE GIFTS!

HARLEQUIN®

Blaze®

red-hot reads!

YES! Please send me 2 FREE Harlequin® Blaze™ novels and my 2 FREE gifts (gifts are worth about $10). After receiving them, if I don't wish to receive any more books, I can return the shipping statement marked "cancel." If I don't cancel, I will receive 4 brand-new novels every month and be billed just $4.74 per book in the U.S. or $4.96 per book in Canada. That's a savings of at least 14% off the cover price. It's quite a bargain. Shipping and handling is just 50¢ per book in the U.S. and 75¢ per book in Canada.* I understand that accepting the 2 free books and gifts places me under no obligation to buy anything. I can always return a shipment and cancel at any time. Even if I never buy another book, the two free books and gifts are mine to keep forever.

150/350 HDN F4WC

Name _____
(PLEASE PRINT)

Address _____ Apt. # _____

City _____ State/Prov. _____ Zip/Postal Code _____

Signature (if under 18, a parent or guardian must sign) _____

Mail to the **Harlequin® Reader Service:**
IN U.S.A.: P.O. Box 1867, Buffalo, NY 14240-1867
IN CANADA: P.O. Box 609, Fort Erie, Ontario L2A 5X3

Want to try two free books from another line?
Call 1-800-873-8635 or visit www.ReaderService.com.

* Terms and prices subject to change without notice. Prices do not include applicable taxes. Sales tax applicable in N.Y. Canadian residents will be charged applicable taxes. Offer not valid in Quebec. This offer is limited to one order per household. Not valid for current subscribers to Harlequin Blaze books. All orders subject to credit approval. Credit or debit balances in a customer's account(s) may be offset by any other outstanding balance owed by or to the customer. Please allow 4 to 6 weeks for delivery. Offer available while quantities last.

Your Privacy—The Harlequin® Reader Service is committed to protecting your privacy. Our Privacy Policy is available online at www.ReaderService.com or upon request from the Harlequin Reader Service.

We make a portion of our mailing list available to reputable third parties that offer products we believe may interest you. If you prefer that we not exchange your name with third parties, or if you wish to clarify or modify your communication preferences, please visit us at www.ReaderService.com/consumerchoice or write to us at Harlequin Reader Service Preference Service, P.O. Box 9062, Buffalo, NY 14269. Include your complete name and address.

HB13R2

"I'm a pro." Kelly laughed. "I surf professionally. At least, I did until a few months ago when I hit Pause and bought this place."

If she'd earned enough to afford this luxury resort, she must have done well as an athlete.

Rafe chastised himself for staring at her, but stopping wasn't an option. He searched his brain to remember what they'd been talking about. "Why'd you hit Pause?"

"To reevaluate, decide what to do next with my life. Burnouts happen and to be honest, I was heading that way. I forgot my love for surfing and I wanted to remember why I've been so dedicated for so long. And it's helped. I can't wait for my next meet." She pursed her lips. "Listen to me. I sound like some weirdo trying to find herself."

"No, you don't," Rafe said quickly. "I love being a marine, but there are days I want to give it up and be a farmer or something."

She grinned. Her amusement pleased him. "You don't seem like the farmer type."

"That *would* be funny, since I've never been on a farm before," he admitted. "But, you know, a job where you work